THE ORPHAN OF HIGHGATE HILL

VICTORIAN ROMANCE

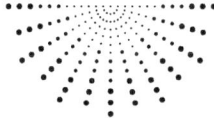

ROSIE SWAN

PUREREAD.COM

CONTENTS

PROLOGUE

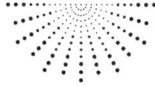

1 *842*

When Mrs Arabella Simpson's second husband died, she did not despair. She was, by then, well-accustomed to the routines of mourning. She took out her cape from her armoire and put it right on without airing it first (she didn't mind the smell of mothballs the way some others did). She ordered her servants to leave all her letters of condolence in a bowl in the vestibule, where she would read them once she was through the throes of grief (she had no intention of doing so, and was only waiting for a moment when she could discreetly dispose of the useless things). She declared that she would not be receiving any visitors for the foreseeable future (which did not make any difference to the servants, since even when her husband was alive, Mrs Simpson had very seldom received visitors).

Apart from these few outward rituals, the death of Mr Andrew Simpson made barely a ripple on his household. He had only been on nodding terms with the servants, having spent most of his time downtown in his club. The house in Highgate, while nominally his, was Mrs Simpson's in every other sense: after their marriage, she had decorated the place according to her own taste, and, as she was wont to boast to others, had really made something of it. It was thanks to her that the newest model of pianoforte had replaced the harpsichord in the drawing room (at least, that particular model of piano *had* been new in 1825, when it had first been installed there) and that the portraits of her husband's eminent ancestors had been moved from an upstairs room to the gallery downstairs, where they might more immediately greet any unsuspecting visitor and force upon them a sense of awe and grandeur.

Mrs Simpson would never have been so brazen as to say it outright, but there had been some, at the time of her second marriage, who had been of the opinion that she had only chosen her new husband for his house, and this was not entirely untrue. Of course, Mr Simpson had come pretty well out of the deal, too, since his wife's money had lifted him out of debt and enabled him to keep said house in the first place. The house's location, in the leafy suburbs of Highgate, had been a definite improvement on the Islington townhouse where Mr Russell had resided until his death, and where the then Mrs Russell had been forced to struggle on for two more years until chance had thrown her in the path of Mr Simpson.

She had been married to Mr Russell for seven years; she had been married to Mr Simpson for seventeen, and yet it was the first husband and not the second who had made much more of an impression on Mrs Simpson. It was only Mr Russell whom she could talk of, after his death, with something resembling affection. This was, presumably, not just due to the twenty thousand pounds that he had left her in his will, but due to the fond memories that she still held of their courtship. In the London scene of the 1810s where the young Miss Lewis had made her debut, Mr Russell had been its most distinguished bachelor. Rich, handsome, well-bred, he had not lacked for marital prospects. But neither had Miss Lewis – beautiful, accomplished, charming – and when these two dazzling young people, these leaders of the fashionable scene, had promised themselves to one another, it seemed one of those rare moments where all the elements of the universe were perfectly aligned. Their wedding was the event of the season.

Miss Lewis had not been lacking for money as a debutante, and she became richer still upon becoming

Mrs Russell. The fact that she was a merchant's daughter had never really been held against her; the London scene had always been willing to overlook such unfortunate origins, provided that those in possession of them made their own valuable contributions to society, and had virtues enough to make it possible to overlook such imperfections. Just as a couple of little freckles could not be said to ruin a lady's otherwise perfect complexion, the source of Miss Lewis's fortune could not be counted against her. She talked and acted just as she was supposed to – just as everyone else did – she always dressed in the latest fashions; she was beautiful, and charming. Yes, she was often said to be 'charming' in those days, and her various accomplishments were praised to high heaven.

Now, at the distance of twenty-six years, Mrs Simpson had lost quite a number of those things that had made her 'win' Mr Russell – a word that she often used, quite proudly, to describe this dazzling courtship. She was no longer accomplished; she had not lifted the lid of her pianoforte, or picked up her watercolours, in at least twenty years. And, worst of all, she was no longer beautiful, either. As she stood before the looking-glass now, on the point of departing for Mr Simpson's funeral, her ever-alert eyes scanned her own face. Her features still had distinction; her fair hair had not yet gone grey, and the black crape set off her pale skin quite well. She had fewer wrinkles than most women her age – but still, at forty-seven, she could only be called 'handsome', not beautiful, and Mrs Simpson turned away from her own reflection in disgust.

It was early December, and frost had made hard points of the grass in Southgate graveyard, gleaming in the sunlight as the minister pronounced his prayers. There was only a small group of mourners: Mr Simpson's sister Elizabeth, a few friends from his club, and some of Mrs Simpson's in-laws from her first marriage. There had been no children, either in Mrs Simpson's second marriage or her first. *That* was a point that had caused some bitterness for her in the past – but Mrs Simpson reflected now that she was glad, since children would only have spoiled the beautiful furniture in her house in Highgate.

She was just congratulating herself on that last piece of good sense when she glimpsed a child, peeking around one of the headstones to watch the funeral. The child was a girl, dressed in rags and barefoot, and evidently shy, for under Mrs Simpson's gaze, she quickly vanished behind the headstone again. Concluding that she must be the gravedigger's daughter, Mrs Simpson thought no more about it, and was being escorted out of the graveyard a half-hour later when the sounds of a commotion made her draw back again.

The gravedigger was remonstrating with that same little girl, who, it seemed from the way he was talking, was not, in fact, his daughter. "Go on, get out of here! I've told you before not to come hanging around here, where you're in the way!"

The girl said something in response, too low for Mrs Simpson to make out, and then held something up in her small white hands. Mrs Simpson's surprised eyes caught the gleam of silver in the sunlight. But the gravedigger looked unimpressed.

"That's not going to help you one bit if you don't have their names. Besides, how do I even know that thing's yours – you might have nicked it!"

Mrs Simpson's patent boots crunched over the frost-tipped grass as she approached the gravedigger and the little girl. Behind her, she could sense the other mourners halting, looking back uncertainly.

"What is this?" asked Mrs Simpson once she was a few paces away from the gravedigger. She looked from him to the little girl, and back again.

The gravedigger, resting a hand on his shovel, glanced at his workmates before replying, a little sheepishly, "Well, ma'am, she's always hanging about here, this little one, saying she's looking for her parents..."

"Your parents?" Mrs Simpson said, looking to the little girl, who nodded eagerly and held up her hands. Now Mrs Simpson could see that the silver object was a locket. It had been prised open, enough to show that there was a little picture inside. Mrs Simpson held out her own black-gloved hand. "May I?"

The girl hesitated for a moment, and then handed the locket over. Mrs Simpson's alert eyes scanned the miniature of the couple that was inside. It was difficult to make out their features, on such a small scale, but they looked fairly well-dressed, and the woman had dark hair like the girl's. Mrs Simpson snapped the locket closed and handed it back down to the girl. "Who told you that your parents are buried here?"

"Aunt Martha," answered the girl after a moment, in such a tone as suggested that this was a person everyone should know. "She showed me... once... but now I've forgotten their names, and I can't find their grave."

"Forgotten? Forgotten your own parents' names?"

"I was very little when Aunt Martha showed me their grave," said the girl, by way of explanation.

"And haven't you asked her since?"

"I... can't." The girl looked down.

Mrs Simpson nodded slowly. "Your aunt died, too?"

"She didn't die," said the girl, almost mumbling now, "She just left."

The gravedigger chose this moment to interject, looking at Mrs Simpson. "It's like I said, ma'am. She's always hanging about here, this little one." He nodded to the girl. "They let her sleep in the church sometimes. I don't believe she has anywhere else to go."

Mrs Simpson did not nod or even meet the man's gaze; she gave no sign at all that she had heard his words. She just held out her hand again and said, "Little girl. Would you like to come home with me?"

1
NOT LONG FOR THIS WORLD

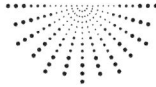

1 *850*

Ned was eleven years old when he made his first journey to London, on his own, to visit his uncle Perry.

His mother put him on the train at Durham and stayed on the platform to wave him off. Ned burrowed down a bit in his seat, and pulled his cap lower over his forehead as he lifted one hand in a surreptitious goodbye. He didn't know what Mum was making such a fuss about; he would only be gone two weeks, and she was the one who had arranged this visit in the first place. She wanted Ned to study law when he was older, and thought that a visit to his solicitor uncle would be a first step in the direction towards that fine ambition. Dad, on the other hand, had made no secret of his disapproval of the trip to London, which he suspected would give Ned "notions". He saw no reason why Ned shouldn't join him in the mine, once he was old enough. But Ned's mother, who had always thought that her eldest son was the brightest of all their children, had recently been strengthened in that conviction by a talk with Ned's teacher, and she would not be gainsaid. Ned's little brothers could follow in their father's footsteps, if they wished; Ned had been marked out for his own special destiny.

Mr Perry was waiting for him at King's Cross station. He was a diminutive, colourless kind of man, who shuffled rather than walked, and who frowned a great deal more than he actually spoke. Ned had never met his mother's brother before, and was not so sure that he would have remembered him even if he had. It was Uncle Perry who approached him on the platform, and who directed him with quiet efficiency out of the crowded station.

"My office is on the South Bank," he informed Ned, as though this piece of London geography would mean anything to him. "It is not raining, so we shall walk."

Ned was surprised to see that the great crowds of people did not drop off, the farther he and his uncle got from King's Cross station, but actually seemed to grow. He wondered where they could all be going. On that long walk, he saw so many faces, wrinkled and freckled, dark and pale, smiling and scowling; so many stories and lives seemed to graze past himself and his uncle before passing swiftly on. Those tall, tall buildings all around seemed to have their own stories, too; Ned craned his neck up to look at them so often that he started to feel stiff.

They passed over the Thames, and Mr Perry began to point out, in a dispassionate voice, various landmarks to his nephew. To Ned's right, around the curve of the river, were the Houses of Parliament. To his left, in the far distance, was London Bridge, which was not, contrary to what schoolyard rhymes would have had him believe, falling down. "And you can't see it now," Uncle Perry said, waving a hand towards the great collection of chimney-stacks that fell away behind them, on the north side of the river, "but St Paul's is there, too."

With all this, Ned was beginning to feel like *he* was in a story, too, and not just surrounded by them. He was ahead of most boys his age (at least, in Durham) when it came to reading, and there was a particular thrill that came with finally seeing places that he had so often read about: places that had been there long before their existence had been set down in print. He wouldn't have minded lingering on the bridge to look at the views, but there was a great tide of people sweeping him on – and Uncle Perry, too, who hadn't even looked around to check that Ned was still behind him, was hurrying on.

Mr Perry's apartment was right above his office, and Ned was shown first one and then the other without finding much to interest him in either. They just appeared to him as a series of dark, stuffy rooms. In one of these rooms,

Mr Perry introduced him to his housekeeper, Miss Pleasant, who laughed when Ned doffed his cap to her and said it had been a long time since she had met any young boys with such good manners. Ned didn't know why good manners should be so funny; his mother was always so insistent that he should practise them, and he was only doing what he had been taught to do.

"I'm sure you must be tired," said his uncle, "so you may go and rest. Tomorrow, you may come to my office and watch me work."

~

Ned knew, by the end of three days, what he had suspected to be true from the moment Uncle Perry had greeted him at King's Cross: that the law was an extremely dull business, so dull that those who chose it as a profession obviously could not prevent its dullness from seeping into their own selves. Watching from his stool in the corner of the office, while his uncle sat behind a desk writing a letter, Ned wondered if it was possible that the man had ever been young. He could not imagine him laughing, or dancing or playing games.

Mr Perry had a clerk, named Frank Allen, a freckly faced fellow who was only a few years older than Ned, and who was so tall and gangly that his head brushed the ceiling of the office. Frank copied out Mr Perry's letters, addressed envelopes and carried messages for him across town, and did all of this with such a bad grace that Ned imagined he must find the work unbearably dull, too. He had to fall back on his imagination in this case, because since the older boy preferred to ignore Ned's existence most of the time, he could not ask him to confirm this theory.

Towards the end of that third day of shadowing Mr Perry, when evening was beginning to draw in and Ned was resigning himself to another evening of sitting in his uncle's parlour, watching the housekeeper trying to light a fire, Frank returned from an errand in town with a note in his hand. "I just met Mrs Simpson's servant downstairs, sir, and he gave me this."

The significance of the name was lost on Ned, but he did see that the sound of it made his uncle sit up straighter at his desk. After squinting at the note for a minute, Mr Perry called his clerk back into the office and said, "I'll be going to Highgate now to attend to this."

"Nothing serious, I hope, sir?" said Frank, with just a hint of eagerness in his voice.

"No, but Mrs Simpson is not someone to be kept waiting." Mr Perry creaked across the office floor, taking his coat and hat from the hooks by the door. "Please finish those invoices while I'm gone. And tell Miss Pleasant not to light the fire yet. And –" He stopped, now on the threshold, and turned back, as did Frank; both had evidently forgotten about Ned, who was still sitting in the corner of the office. "And, my nephew..."

"Can I come with you?" asked Ned.

Mr Perry blinked, as though the thought had never occurred to him. "Well – I suppose you can. I don't think Mrs Simpson would object. She has a daughter around your age – maybe you can play together while we are settling business."

The prospect of the evening was looking brighter and brighter for Ned, with each word that came out of his uncle's mouth. He practically leapt off his stool, picking up his cap and fustian jacket from the same set of hooks where Mr Perry had taken his things. But as he was about to follow his uncle over the threshold, Frank grabbed the sleeve of his jacket to pull him back.

"She's not really her daughter," he said, in a whisper. "They say she pulled her off the streets."

"Who?" said Ned, too surprised by the fact that the clerk was talking to him to be able to make much sense of what he was saying.

"I mean the girl who lives with Mrs Simpson." Frank widened his eyes significantly. "They call her Miss Smith – but that's only because no one really knows who her parents were, least of all her. But she's got such airs, as if her blood was as blue as the Queen's!"

"Is she pretty?" said Ned, intrigued.

"Oh yes." Frank nodded solemnly. "And doesn't she know it! Doesn't she know it..."

Mr Perry's voice echoed from outside, calling for his nephew, and Ned was forced to depart without asking any more of the questions that were burning on his lips.

He got the feeling that Frank had been trying to scare him away from talking to Miss Smith, especially with those ominous last words, but if that *had* been the young clerk's intention, it had had just the opposite effect. At this, the first prospect of excitement in days, Ned's whole being had lit up, and he once again felt like he had when crossing the Thames with Mr Perry: like a boy in one of the stories that he loved to read, uncertain what fate would unfold on the pages ahead, and revelling in that uncertainty. On the cab journey to Mrs Simpson's house, Ned imagined a great many different ways in which his meeting with Miss Smith would play out; he had leisure to do so, because Mr Perry was completely silent, having taken out some papers from his valise which completely absorbed him.

The leafy avenues of Highgate, then, which they drove through, and the freshness of the air pouring in the carriage window, added to Ned's excitement, because this environment provided such a contrast from the narrow streets of the South Bank, and the smoky alleys of Durham. Every house that they passed seemed bigger than the last, and at every gate, he sat up straighter, expecting them to stop. When they finally did stop, it was in front of a house set back further from the road then the others, and so surrounded by trees as to be partly obscured from view.

Mr Perry paid the cab driver and stepped out behind Ned, who had already leapt down onto the path and was fixing his cap onto his head. They rang the bell, and were waiting for some minutes before the figure of a maidservant emerged through the trees. She greeted Mr Perry and ignored Ned, who had smiled tentatively at her – he was glad then, remembering Miss Pleasant's amusement, that he had refrained from bowing this time. The gate opened with a long creak that sounded almost like a human cry.

"Miss Simpson and Mr Morgan are here too," the maid informed Mr Perry as she led them up the drive. Mr Perry made a noise that suggested that this news was of some vague interest to him; Ned, meanwhile, only registered a flash of curiosity regarding the unfamiliar names, for he was otherwise occupied in peering up at the house. With each step they took, more and more of it emerged from behind the trees. He saw a red brick facade, in places obscured with creeping ivy, and many dark windows. The place looked to be at least a hundred years old, and some of the trees that they passed, judging by their gnarled trunks, were even older. Hearing squelching under his boots, Ned looked down and saw that he was treading in mulch: there were piles and piles of rotting leaves on the drive that no one seemed to have bothered to clear away. No one even seemed to notice them except for him. At the front door, he wiped his soles carefully on the mat, worried about tracking in dirt.

Indoors, it appeared to already be night, even though it was still light outside. They passed through a dark, musty-smelling hall and into a gallery that was well-lit: candles had been placed at intervals on tables set back against the wall, and their flickering light illuminated the numerous portraits overhead. Ned, much impressed, turned this way and that to look at each one. He wondered if the people in them were related to Mrs Simpson or to her husband. It struck him that it was a very fine thing, to have ancestors.

"Watch your step here," said the maid, taking up one of the candles as she led the way out of the gallery, and Ned soon saw what she meant. They passed from comparative brightness into pitch-dark once more: through the small circle of light thrown by the maid's candle, he saw a staircase stretching up ahead. Mr Perry began to climb at once, evidently used to navigating its steps in dimness, as he seemed to know exactly where to place his feet. Ned, on the other hand, stumbled more than once, and the third time, the maid halted and waited until he had caught up with her. "Stay close to me," she said, with something like sympathy in her voice. Then, in an undertone, "The mistress prefers to save on candles where she can."

"She is very economical," said Mr Perry, who had overheard, and as the admiration in his voice was clear, the maid subsided into silence. Ned, as he followed behind, wondered why Mrs Simpson had so many candles lit downstairs in the gallery, if she was worried about saving money.

On the upstairs landing, a chink of light under one of the doors, and the sound of soft female voices from within, told Ned that they had come to the drawing room. The maid made them wait until she had opened the door and announced them first, but it only seemed to occur to her then that she was unaware of Ned's name. "Mr Perry and –" She looked back at the visitors questioningly.

"Edward Hyland, my nephew," Mr Perry said, and the maid, with an uncertain expression, repeated the name.

"Come in," came a lady's voice, which sounded so young that Ned was surprised to find, as they entered the drawing room, that its owner was a lady of more mature years. He assumed that this must be Mrs Simpson. She had no lace cap on as ladies of her age tended to wear. Her hair, instead, was fastened above the nape of her neck in an old-fashioned style, with a few curls hanging loose around her face. In the firelight, its shade might have been fair or light grey; it was difficult to tell. She was dressed in half-mourning, the black shawl around her shoulders long enough to reach the floor from her chair, where its ends mingled with the folds of her mauve gown. The hands resting in her lap were soft and white, as though they had never seen a day's wear in their life. Only her eyes gave her away; Ned's first emotion, upon meeting them, was one of pity, because they were eyes that looked weary with life; eyes that told him that nothing he could say or do would be of any interest or surprise.

On a footstool close to Mrs Simpson's armchair was not Miss Smith, as Ned had expected, but a woman who appeared closer to Mrs Simpson's age; where the latter sat idle, however, this woman was all activity. Her clicking needles had not slowed upon the entrance of the visitors; she appeared to be knitting a scarf. Ned wondered how she could see her work with Mrs Simpson blocking the firelight. The curtains had already been drawn and tied over the windows – as he was also to learn later, it was routine in the house in Highgate that, regardless of the season, the maid would always draw the curtains at five o'clock in the evening. Those windows were seldom opened, either, if the warm, stagnant air in the drawing room was any indication.

And while that stagnant air did not appear to have affected either Mrs Simpson or the other woman adversely, the third member of their party – a girl who, with a throb of his boyish heart, Ned knew must be Miss Smith – was nearly asleep. She was sitting backwards at the piano in the corner of the room, leaning against its closed lid, her head lolling to one side. A sketchbook was gripped loosely in one of her hands, and its accompanying pencil had already fallen to the floor. Her neat ringlets had begun to go limp from the warmth, and dark tendrils of hair clung to the edges of her forehead; her eyelashes, dark against her flushed cheeks, fluttered a little under

Ned's gaze, and he quickly looked away before he could be caught staring.

But while he was quick enough to avoid being seen by Miss Smith, he had drawn the attention of another. Mrs Simpson's eyes, steadily watching Ned all this time, now had a flicker of amusement in them. "Master Edward," she said, considering. "Your uncle never mentioned you before."

"Please, ma'am, everyone calls me Ned."

The lady's face twitched, as though in danger of breaking into a smile. "And who is 'everyone'?"

"My mother and father and brothers and sisters," Ned mumbled, all too aware now that there were several pairs of eyes on him. Out of the corner of his eye, he saw Miss Smith stirring on her stool. "And... other people 'round town."

"Town? And what town is that? I can't decipher your accent. Is it Manchester, Newcastle, Preston?"

"Durham, ma'am," said Mr Perry, with a cough.

"Durham... the place with the mines?"

"Aye, ma'm, that's the one," said Ned, and though he saw nothing very strange in what he had said, it made Miss Smith break into peals of laughter.

"'Aye ma'm, that's the one,'" she mimicked, and then put a hand over her mouth as fresh waves of mirth seized her.

In between giggles, "I can see the coal dust on his trousers!"

This struck Ned as unfair, since he knew his mother had taken great care in washing those trousers, and it was not her fault if, in one or two places, the material had come into contact with his father's mining clothes. But he had already made up his mind to love Miss Smith, and a contemptuous remark was not going to sway him.

"Now, now, Beatrice," said Mrs Simpson mildly, while the woman beside her paused in her knitting to look over her shoulder at Miss Smith and ask pointedly,

"Have you finished your sketch of Mr Morgan yet?"

"No," replied Beatrice – Ned's whole being thrilled, now that he knew the first name of his beloved – and, with a defiant lift of her chin, she adjusted her grip on her sketchbook. "I don't see how I'm supposed to sketch him when he's out of the room."

"You might sketch him from memory," retorted the woman with the knitting needles. "Many artists do."

"And how would *you* know what artists do, Eliza Simpson?" Beatrice said, with a disbelieving laugh.

"Beatrice," said Mrs Simpson again, in the same mild tone, and though the utterance had the effect of silencing her ward, it had no other effect – at least, none that Ned could observe. The full force of young Beatrice's contempt was now directed at the woman named Eliza Simpson, where it had been directed at Ned moments before, and she did not appear at all sorry or ashamed to have spoken in such a way in front of strangers. The clicking of Miss Simpson's needles went on uninterrupted, although Ned could see that she had turned red at the younger girl's words.

"I suppose you know who I am," Mrs Simpson said to Ned after a moment's pause. Her gaze flickered to Mr Perry, who was still standing in the same posture that he had adopted upon entering the room, his hat in hand and his diminutive frame hunched in on itself so as to appear even smaller. "I suppose your uncle told you."

"Yes, Mrs Simpson, ma'am," Ned said, and, judging it to be the right time at last, he bowed. When he straightened up again a moment later, he saw, with relief that his hostess had not erupted into laughter the way Miss Pleasant had done. She looked unsurprised, bored once more, as with a small gesture of one hand she indicated her companions.

"This is my sister-in-law Miss Elizabeth Simpson. She resides in Dover, but was kind enough to make the journey to London today for no other reason than the pleasure of seeing me."

"It is nothing to me," said Miss Simpson at once, pausing in her knitting, "indeed, I would make the journey every day if you were to ask me to. I could do nothing less, for one who was so dear to my brother Andrew..."

"Let's not get carried away," Mrs Simpson interrupted, and Ned saw that the thin, sardonic smile on her face was replicated exactly on that of Beatrice, to whom their hostess now turned her attention. "And this is my ward, Beatrice Smith. She is about your age, I suppose, Master Ned?"

"I'm sure I'm much older than *him*," said Beatrice, the smile vanishing from her face as suddenly as it had appeared. "He's so small!"

"What age are you?" Mrs Simpson asked Ned.

"Eleven, ma'am," said Ned quietly.

"And Beatrice has just turned thirteen. So not such a great difference after all."

"Why –" Beatrice began, flushing red in indignation, but she was silenced once more by a glance from her guardian.

"That was precisely my thinking," Mr Perry said hastily, "which is why, ma'am, I thought you might not object to my bringing Edward here today. He is staying with me for a fortnight, to learn something of my profession. His mother intends him to study it when he is older."

"Does she." Mrs Simpson's tone was so flat and indifferent that it was hard to recognise what she had said as a question at all. "Well, since he can observe very little now – our business being of a confidential nature – he will do better as Beatrice's playmate for today. It is so rare that she gets to see people of her own age."

"I don't *want* to –"

"My cousin, James, is in the garden undertaking some repairs to the wall of the house," Mrs Simpson continued, as though Beatrice had not spoken. "He is very useful in that respect. Go fetch him back, Beatrice, and bring Master Ned with you. Miss Simpson will go too."

"I had much rather stay..." murmured her sister-in-law.

"Miss Simpson will go, too," repeated Mrs Simpson, and with one last click of her needles, her sister-in-law rose reluctantly from her chair. She strode to the door without a glance towards either of the children, and stepped out. Ned waited until Beatrice had passed by, with a ruffle of skirts and a contemptuous, sweeping glance, and then followed them out of the drawing room, leaving Mrs Simpson and Mr Perry to their own private conference.

∾

There were no young girls back in Durham whom Ned knew enough to compare them with Beatrice, but all the same, he had felt from his first glimpse of her that she was something out of the ordinary, and this impression was only strengthened by their time alone together. Mr Morgan being nowhere in sight when they had come out into the garden, Miss Simpson had excused herself to go find him, and Ned and Beatrice were left on their own for a few minutes.

It was twilight, the overgrown grass damp beneath their feet, and Ned heard Beatrice drawing in deep breaths of the evening air as though desperate to fill her lungs as quickly as possible before they had to go back inside. She had been silent on their walk through the darkened house, but now she began to talk easily to Ned, with none of the crossness that she had shown before. Her eyes had brightened like stars, and even the material of her grey dress, which had been wrinkled and limp upstairs in the drawing room, seemed to revive, taking on its own strange gleam. It was of an old-fashioned design, with leg-of-mutton sleeves and a bell-shaped skirt, but to Ned's eyes this only seemed to add to Beatrice's charm; in her funny dress, she looked all the more like she had stepped out of the pages of one of his books.

"What's it like to work in a mine?" was one of her first questions, and when Ned told her, regretfully, that he didn't know as he had never been inside one himself, she was more than content to listen to a second-hand account of the conditions, as described to Ned by Ned's father.

"And so the canary stops singing when the air is bad," she said thoughtfully. "And that's all it's used for. How sad."

"It doesn't always die," Ned assured her. "They try to get out in time so that it won't. Because if the canary dies –"

"*They* might die, too," Beatrice finished, with a drop in her voice that made a chill run up Ned's neck. She gazed off to the side for a moment, and then said, "My parents are dead."

"I'm sorry," Ned said uncertainly.

"I wonder," Beatrice went on in the same strange voice, "how they must feel, buried so deep down with all that earth above them. I wonder if your father feels the same, when he goes down to work in the mine."

Ned couldn't help the shudder that ran through him. "You shouldn't talk like that."

"Why not?" Beatrice demanded.

"Because it's not true. Your parents aren't down there. They're in a better place – in..."

"Heaven?" Beatrice finished scornfully. Ned nodded, though suddenly he was finding it hard to meet her gaze. "You don't know what it's like," she went on. "It's easy for you to say that, when your parents are alive. But how can you be sure, if they died, whether they would go to heaven?"

"Because that's what we're taught," said Ned in a low voice. "That if you live a good life..."

"What if they haven't lived good lives?"

"But they have. My mum and dad –"

"I'm not talking about your 'mum and dad', I'm talking about mine." Beatrice sighed. "I think you might be the stupidest boy I've ever met."

"I'm sure your parents lived good lives, too," Ned said, ignoring this.

"Stupider and stupider," Beatrice marvelled. The thin smile that seemed far too old for her had appeared on her face once again. "How do you think I ended up here, Ned Hyland? My parents didn't want me: they left me to starve. If Mrs Simpson hadn't found me, I'd have died on the streets."

Ned, moved by pity to silence, took a few moments to form a response. "When was that? When did she find you?"

"Oh, I don't know anymore." Beatrice shrugged, evidently weary of their conversation. "I feel I've always lived with her, somehow. Come, let's see where Eliza Simpson has got herself to. Snooping around the pantry no doubt. You know she hopes to own this place someday?" She carried on talking over her shoulder to Ned as they went back inside. "As if Mrs Simpson would ever put her in her will, let alone give her this house. Eliza Simpson can travel up from Dover every day if she likes, but it won't change that fact. She – "

Beatrice stopped short, for to their left a baize door had just swung open and a young gentleman had stepped out into their path. He was swarthy, with a well-trimmed beard and pale blue eyes. "Speaking ill of your elders, are you, Miss Smith?" he asked with a smirk.

"Mr Morgan," stammered Beatrice, and Ned saw, with a sidelong glance at her, that she had gone red. "This is Ned Hyland. Ned, this is Mr James Morgan, Mrs Simpson's cousin."

"Cousin?" Ned repeated, a little doubtfully, for the man looked significantly younger than Mrs Simpson.

"First cousin once removed," Mr Morgan said, only sparing a cursory glance at Ned before turning his blue gaze back on Beatrice. "Or is it twice? I never can remember."

"It's once removed," Beatrice said distractedly. "I've heard Mrs Simpson say it many times. Your mother is her first cousin, the child of her mother's younger sister. Mr Morgan, what were you doing in the servants' stairs? You know that we've been sent with Miss Simpson to summon you back."

"Yes, I'm aware," said Mr Morgan, still smirking. "having just come across that good woman myself. I've sent her back up to Mrs Simpson, and now I'll send you two back, too, before you can get in any more trouble." There was something in the way that, upon uttering that last word, he inclined his head and lowered his voice, that made Ned's gut tighten. Another sidelong glance at Beatrice showed him that her blush had deepened. Mr Morgan went on, "And I'll give you the same message that I gave her: that before my repairs to the wall can be finished, there is a dampness issuing from the pipes in the kitchen that needs my immediate attention. It will take another few hours, at least, to discover its source, as the servants are not being especially helpful in that regard."

"Then you won't be coming up for tea?" The dismay in Beatrice's voice was evident.

"I'm afraid you'll have to do without me today, Miss Smith."

"But surely Mrs Simpson can hire someone to do all this," Beatrice protested. "It doesn't seem right..."

"It's perfectly right that I should make myself useful to Mrs Simpson," Mr Morgan told her, "just as you do, in your own way. Now off you go."

Beatrice was silent all the way back to the drawing room. When they entered, Miss Simpson had resumed her former place on the footstool by her sister-in-law's chair, while Mr Perry, though he had consented to sit, had evidently made the compromise between comfort and professionalism by choosing one of the hardest chairs in the room, and posting himself at the very edge of its seat.

It had been a while since Ned had eaten. But the entrance of the tea-tray brought no excitement; he barely tasted the bread-and-butter and his tea went cold, because across the room he could see Beatrice, who had returned to her piano-stool and to her sketching, undertaking the latter with a new energy and resolve. Since Mrs Simpson did not enforce her attending them to tea, neither of the other grown-ups mentioned her absence, and at length Beatrice put down her sketchbook and strolled over to the table, helping herself to one of the last pieces of cake. Ned's intent eyes followed her all the time, as she ate her cake and then walked over to the window, staring moodily out at the growing dark.

"May we look at your sketch, Beatrice?" said Miss Simpson, and Beatrice gave an indistinct reply that suggested her indifference as to whether they did or not. Eagerly Miss Simpson went over and picked up the sketchbook, flipping to the right page. Ned was no less eager when she returned to the tea-table, craning his neck so that he could see what Beatrice had drawn. When Miss Simpson turned the book around, he was not really surprised by what he saw, but his heart sank all the same. It was, in very flattering lines, a sketch of Mr Morgan, wearing just the same self-satisfied expression that he had had when Ned and Beatrice had come across him a little while ago.

"It is a very good likeness." Miss Simpson gave the praise with an air of reluctance. "Is it not?" Mr Perry nodded his assent, though he had only glanced at the sketch. Mrs Simpson was next pressed for her opinion.

"Yes, it is good," she said measuredly, looking over the sketch, "and drawing is all very well, in its way, but I think to play an instrument is much more attractive in a young lady. Of course, at Beatrice's age I could do both. But I don't expect her to be like I was – still, it is a pity she does not practise her piano enough." Beatrice, still gazing out the window, showed no signs of hearing.

"I would dearly love to hear you play again, ma'am," said Miss Simpson fervently. "I remember when you first had that lovely instrument brought here – what a stir it made! And how Andrew enjoyed sitting and listening to you..."

"Oh, he cared nothing for my playing," Mrs Simpson said scornfully. "He hardly knew Beethoven from Mozart. Not like Theo – Theo could play almost as well as I did."

There was a silence. Miss Simpson, who had been gazing at her hostess just moments before, suddenly averted her gaze. "Who is Theo?" Ned asked, after the pause had become long enough to be almost unbearable. No one answered him.

Mr Perry announced that they were to take their leave a few minutes later. With an air of conferring a great favour, Mrs Simpson held out one of her hands for Ned to kiss. "You must come and visit us again soon," she told him, "I'm sure Beatrice would like it."

Beatrice, standing at the window, still had her back to them, and had not said a word. With a glance at her, Ned looked back at Mrs Simpson and said, "But I'll only be in London for two weeks."

"What, and leave us so soon? When we were just getting acquainted with you!" There was a gleam of something in Mrs Simpson's eyes, mockery or mere amusement; Ned could not tell which. Uncertain of what to say, he just bowed.

"You must come often, for as long as you are here," Mrs Simpson pursued. "I'm sure I can spin out my business with Mr Perry for longer, if an excuse is needed – though I shouldn't have thought any excuse necessary to visit myself and my ward." Her significant glance at Beatrice, and then back at Ned, made her meaning clear enough.

"No, of course it isn't necessary," Ned babbled. "I have enjoyed myself very much and it would be my pleasure to come again."

As they were leaving the drawing room, he glanced back one last time, without being sure what he had expected or hoped to see. He saw only the back of Beatrice's dark head; she had made no move, nor uttered a single word to acknowledge their parting.

Out in the passage, they bumped into Mr Morgan, who, rather than continuing into the drawing room, insisted on attending them downstairs so that he might assist them in ordering a cab. His helpful efforts were more cordially met by Mr Perry than by Ned, who trudged along behind the two men in sullen silence. Mr Morgan had the candle, and so Ned was obliged to keep his eyes trained on him so as not to trip over his own feet in the darkness. But he chafed under the obligation, and glared at Mr Morgan's back; for just as surely as he had decided to love Beatrice Smith that day, he had decided to hate the man whom she so evidently admired.

Out over the rotting leaves and through the creaky gate they were led, and after Mr Morgan had walked a little way up the road and succeeded in summoning a cab, he strode back alongside the conveyance, hovering in attendance for a little longer. Ned soon saw why; the moment Mr Perry went over to the driver to instruct him as to their destination, Mr Morgan seized the opportunity to take Ned by the arm and say into his ear,

"She never mentioned you were Perry's nephew. The little minx. If she had, I would have taken the chance to talk to you properly."

Ned could only assume he was referring to Beatrice, and bristled on her behalf. "Let me go."

"Just a minute, now." Mr Morgan, watching Mr Perry, continued in an undertone, "You must know everything, then, don't you? Who's going to get what."

"I don't," Ned said, struggling to free himself from his grip. "I don't even know what you're talking about."

"If you don't know, you're to find out for me," said Mr Morgan, with decision. He turned to meet Ned's bewildered gaze, and matched it with his own look of incredulity. "Well, you must have heard that the old lady isn't long for this world, at least?"

"I didn't," Ned said, thinking of Mrs Simpson's soft white hands, of the youthful sound of her voice, "and I don't think it's any of my business..."

Here Mr Morgan laughed, so loudly and scornfully that both the cab driver and Mr Perry looked around. "It *is* your business," Mr Morgan said into Ned's ear, "or your uncle's business, at least. I want to know what he knows." Drawing back from Ned before he could protest or argue, Mr Morgan said to Mr Perry, "Just sharing a little joke with your nephew here."

Mr Perry's incurious gaze slid past him. "We had better be getting back, Edward," was all he said, and Ned followed him into the carriage, rubbing the spot on his arm where he could still feel Mr Morgan's vice-like grip.

2

A QUESTION ANSWERED

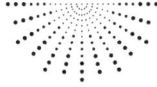

Over the next few days, the clerk Frank Allen dropped his formal manner – namely, of pretending that Ned didn't exist – and became most communicative. Every time Mr Perry left his office, it opened an opportunity for conversation. On the one hand, Frank wanted to hear every detail of Ned's visit to Highgate, and on the other, he proved quite useful in answering whatever questions had arisen from that visit.

"Theo? Why, that would be Mrs Simpson's first husband. Theobald Russell. No wonder Miss Simpson didn't like to hear him mentioned. Everyone knows Mrs Simpson liked him best."

"Mrs Simpson has been married twice?" Ned said. He had a pile of envelopes in front of him that he was supposed to seal and address, but they sat abandoned; Frank, likewise, had paused halfway through copying a letter to deliver this information to Ned.

"Oh, yes. One for ten years and the other for twenty, or something like that. I'm not sure quite how old she is."

Ned hesitated before telling Frank what Mr Morgan had said about Mrs Simpson. "Do you think she could be ill?"

"She must be," Frank said, with a shrug. "Why else would they all be hanging around there all the time? They want to make sure she doesn't forget them in her will. And why else do you think Mr Perry is making house visits?"

"But what about the Russells?" Ned asked. "Didn't you say Mr Russell was her favourite? Surely she'd want to leave his family something."

"He might have been her favourite, but she hasn't spoken to his family in years. They hated her because her father was in trade – they thought Theo could do better."

"How do you know all this?" Ned said after a moment, shaking his head. "It all happened so long ago."

"Her servants know all about it." Frank shrugged. "Some of them are left over from Mr Russell's time. I got talking to them, last time Mr Perry brought me over to her house when he had business there."

Ned glanced towards the door that stood open to the stairs to his uncle's apartment. He could distantly hear Mr

Perry up there, issuing some instructions to Miss Pleasant. "Mr Morgan wants me to find out about the will," he told Frank, a new urgency in his voice. "He wants to know who gets what."

Far from being shocked, Frank just nodded. "Well, of course. He wants to marry Beatrice, once she's old enough. But he needs to know if it's worth his while first. He's poor as a church mouse – he needs something sure to count on."

"So he thinks... that Mrs Simpson is going to settle everything on Beatrice."

"*Everyone* thinks that. She never had any children, after all. Raised Beatrice like she was her own, named her and all." Frank dabbed the pen in the inkstand, held it up at a little height and idly watched the ink drip back down. "Morgan's playing it safe. He hangs around Mrs Simpson enough, makes himself useful enough to her, and maybe she'll remember her cousin and give him something. But even if she doesn't, there's still Beatrice – and if he's in *her* good graces..."

"He is," said Ned in a low voice.

Finally he had said something to surprise Frank. "You think so?" The clerk stared at him. "You think Beatrice will marry him?"

"I know she will," Ned said.

"Maybe you're right. Well, she's not going to marry you, anyway, so I advise you to stop moping. Remember – I've been through it, too. She never even looked at me twice."

"Me neither," said Ned, miserably.

"She thinks she's too good for us. Too good for everyone. And she grew up on the streets! Well –" But here Frank stopped, as the sound of Mr Perry's footsteps echoed down the stairs. They both had their heads down over their work by the time he entered.

"What, not finished yet?" he said mildly. "It'll be dark soon. Frank, you head home and leave the rest for my nephew."

"Thank you, sir." Frank was out of his seat in a flash and picking his coat from the hook beside the door. But as he was about to step over the threshold he paused, and looked back to inquire, "Will you be going to Mrs Simpson's again tomorrow, sir?"

"I think so," Mr Perry said, settling into the seat that Frank had just vacated to take a look at his papers. "She seemed to take a liking to my nephew the last time. Besides, we still have some business to conclude."

"That's good," said Frank. "It will be... good for Mr Hyland to observe what he can – about the profession, I mean. Keep his eyes open." He met Ned's gaze and gave a significant nod. Ned nodded back, a little more uncertainly.

It was something that Ned had never experienced before, being divided between dread and excited anticipation, having one emotion reign over the other seemingly at random, as the hours ticked down before his next visit to Highgate. He wanted to see Beatrice again, more than anything, even if it was just to be ignored by her, even if it was just to be kicked around like dirt under her feet. But the thought of seeing Mr Morgan again, and having to face up to what he had asked him, made Ned's skin crawl. As for Mrs Simpson, Ned wasn't so sure whether he wanted to see her again or not. Knowing more about her past gave him no more insight into her present state.

What had a lady like her to do with her long days, cooped up in that dark house? Did she amuse herself by playing little games with people? Ned remembered the gleam of amusement in her eyes as she had talked to him, during the visit. Was she playing some game with him now, the humble boy from Durham, a town she knew so little about? Suddenly, for the first time since he had come to London, Ned felt a powerful longing for home: for people he knew and understood, who did not mock him for things he could not help. Then, in the next instant, Beatrice's face returned to his mind, and, once more, his desire to see *her* again overpowered all other inclinations.

The visit to Highgate that day was less eventful than the last. Mr Morgan, to Ned's relief, was nowhere to be seen.

Miss Simpson had extended her stay, to the evident displeasure of Mrs Simpson, who inquired more than once of her sister-in-law, within earshot of Ned and Mr Perry, whether the goat she kept in Dover would not be missing her, and who had undertaken to feed him while she was away amusing herself in London. Miss Simpson seemed oblivious to these hints – if "hints" they could even be called – but Beatrice derived much amusement from them, sometimes laughing openly. Ned noted this with regret; it gave him even more pain to see Beatrice's contempt directed at someone else than if it had been directed towards himself, especially since Miss Simpson, as a single woman, Beatrice's elder and her guardian's relation, merited more respect than *he* did. But Mrs Simpson let all of Beatrice's unkindness go unchecked, and was so clearly unconcerned by it that Ned doubted whether, even in private, she ever attempted to improve Beatrice's behaviour the way that a guardian – or parent – should have.

After tea had been cleared, Beatrice agreed to play for the guests, and lifted the piano lid, a cloud of dust rising from its keys. A more impartial observer than Ned would have noted that she was an indifferent player who had attempted a piece far beyond her abilities, and that the performance was saved only by the accompaniment of her good, strong voice. But to Ned's eyes, and, apparently, to the eyes of the rest of the company, the performance was nothing short of perfect, an extension of Beatrice's own charm.

After she had finished playing, Beatrice lowered the lid again and turned around to lean her back against it, taking the comfortable position in which Ned had first seen her. Then she and Mrs Simpson began a conversation in which no one else could really share: a comparison of the merits of certain German or Italian composers over others, a discussion of various operas, operettas and oratorios. Ned was utterly lost. Mr Perry gazed blankly at the wall, and only Miss Simpson seemed to be attempting to follow the conversation, although she soon gave up once Mrs Simpson began talking fondly about her "dear Theo".

Mrs Simpson's first husband, it seemed, had not only been an excellent piano-player but had also possessed a beautiful baritone voice. "Completely untrained," said Mrs Simpson, proudly. "Never had a day of lessons in his life. And yet, to hear him, you would think he had been born for the stage. We often sang duets together at parties, and people loved to listen to us."

Miss Simpson, by this point, had gone red, and Ned saw Beatrice glance at her before continuing to question Mrs Simpson eagerly, "And what kind of songs did you sing together? Was he a good dancer, too? Anyone with a musical ear tends to be. How I wish I could have been acquainted with him!"

Mrs Simpson was only too happy to indulge Beatrice in answering these questions, and the two continued on the same subject for so long, while Miss Simpson got redder and redder, that it became clear they were trying to provoke her. Not a single mention was made of Mr Simpson, of what *his* habits or hobbies had been. Ned, forced to watch all this, got quite angry himself, and when the time came for him and Mr Perry to leave, he made a bow and was on the point of walking out without another word, when Mrs Simpson called him back.

"Dear Ned," she said, holding out her hand for him to kiss just as she had done last time, "We have enjoyed your company so much that I see no need to invent excuses for it anymore. My business with your uncle is done, but you may come back to see us, with or without him, whenever you like. You needn't trouble yourself writing ahead: we will be happy to see you any time."

Since he had barely spoken throughout the whole visit, Ned couldn't see how his company could have been enjoyable or made any impression on them at all, and he saw behind Mrs Simpson's smiling invitation some trick or joke. He thanked her, avoiding Beatrice's gaze, and made his escape from the house gratefully, resolving that he would never step through its creaky gate again. He had had his fill of these people; he had had his fill of the law and London and even Frank Allen, whose eager questions to Ned about Mrs Simpson and her hangers-on, this time around, went unanswered.

But such a resolution was more easily made than kept. Ned dreamt of Beatrice at night, and during the day, faced with whatever tedious task Mr Perry had assigned him, whenever his mind wandered it was always to her. By his last day in London, he had convinced himself – helped along by his uncle's mild reasoning – that while it had been wise for him to stay away from Highgate all this time, since he was not sure whether Mrs Simpson's invitation had been meant or not, there could be no harm in his going there alone to bid them farewell.

He fixed the hour for his visit at noon, since his train to Durham was at six that evening, and, being familiar enough by now with the route to Highgate, set out by himself on foot, two hours in advance. As he walked, the September sun beating down on his cap, the way ahead seemed one dazzling, sunlit thoroughfare, leading straight to Beatrice and to perfect happiness.

He rang the bell at the gate and was waiting for some time before the maid came out, squinting in the sun. "Who are you?" She looked him up and down doubtfully.

"Don't you remember me? I'm Mr Perry's nephew, Ned."

"Oh yes." The maid made no move to open the gate. "Well... are you expected?"

"No," Ned was forced to say, after a moment. "Not exactly. But Mrs Simpson did say I could call any time..."

"Did she?" The maid looked more doubtful still.

"... and I am going back to Durham today so I thought I might say goodbye."

"Hmph. You'd better wait here while I go and ask."

Ned waited obediently, one hand on the rusting bars of the gate and the other wiping the sweat from his brow every now and then. More than one carriage rolled past, and he began to feel more and more conspicuous, standing there in his dusty trousers. They were his good trousers, too, the ones without the coal dust stains, but they had been ruined on his long walk. He was about to go away when he discerned the maid's figure crossing the drive.

Without a word she unlocked the gate and beckoned him to follow her, by which Ned understood that Mrs Simpson must have agreed to the visit. Coming through the house in daylight, he could see that a fine sheen of dust lay over everything, from the handrail on the stairs to the frames of the paintings. The place was evidently cleaned sometimes, but not often enough: certainly not with the daily diligence shown by Ned's mum back in Durham, who would consider a particle of dust on a piece of her furniture as a personal reflection on her character.

Mrs Simpson and Beatrice were in the drawing room, as usual. Beatrice had a book in her lap, and had evidently been reading aloud to her guardian before Ned came in. Seeing that his entrance had interrupted their activity, he felt more awkward still. They informed him that Miss Simpson had gone back to Dover, and that Mr Morgan was somewhere around the house, undertaking some more repairs.

"Tell me something, Ned," Mrs Simpson said, with an air of amusement, once the usual civilities had been exchanged. "Do people often call on each other so early in the day, where you come from?"

"I have my train home this evening," Ned explained, twisting his cap around in his hands. "I thought I might come to say goodbye, before I left. To thank you and... Miss Smith..." He nodded to Beatrice, who was watching him with her eyebrows raised, "... for your – kindness to me."

"Well, I think we must thank *you* in turn for *your* kindness," said Mrs Simpson, smiling, "in remembering our dull selves enough to want to say goodbye. Enough to want to come here *alone*, too, which is a definite mark of our distinction." She looked to her ward, who was also smiling now, too. "We seem to have impressed him, Beatrice, have we not?"

Ned could feel the blood rushing to his face. It seemed either that Mrs Simpson had forgotten her invitation to him last time, or that she had only ever meant it as a joke to begin with; standing there before them now, he could not tell which possibility was worse.

"Do sit down, Ned, and make yourself comfortable. Beatrice has been reading to me one of Mr Dickens' – are you familiar?"

"Yes," said Ned, with some relief, and then, with an anxious glance at Beatrice, "Don't let me interrupt..."

"Oh, no, no, don't trouble yourself," said Mrs Simpson. "We are just as content to discuss as to read aloud – indeed, we often do both. Which of his novels is your favourite, Ned?"

"*Oliver Twist*," Ned replied, and he saw by the smiles they exchanged that it was the very answer they had been expecting.

"One of his earlier works, yes," said Mrs Simpson. "And certainly one of the most *popular*." Somehow she invested the word with so much venom as to make it sound like a positive insult; Ned could almost see the pages of his copy of *Oliver Twist*, on his bed stand back home, withering before his eyes. "We have been reading from *Dombey and Son*."

"I don't know that one," Ned confessed.

"It is one of his newer novels. We are enjoying it very much. It follows a father who values his son over his daughter – nothing she can do will make him take any notice of her."

"He reminds me of the father in *King Lear*," Beatrice said, and Mrs Simpson nodded.

"Yes, perhaps that was an inspiration – but we are forgetting ourselves; our guest may not be as familiar with the bard as we are."

"I've never read *King Lear*," Ned admitted. "Only *Macbeth* and *Romeo and Juliet*." Feeling some need to make up for his lack of knowledge with enthusiasm, he pushed on, "But I think Shakespeare must be the greatest writer who ever lived."

Mrs Simpson and Beatrice exchanged another smile. "Oh, yes, there can be no doubt about that," said the former. "Though some come close. There is Milton, for instance – who could forget his description of Eden in *Paradise Lost*? And Spenser, further back. 'For whatsoever from one place doth fall, is with the tide unto another brought...'"

"'... for there is nothing lost, that may be found, if sought'," finished Beatrice, quietly.

"I like that one," said Ned, much struck.

"Do you? Take note, Beatrice: we must read Spenser next. Our fine critic, Ned Hyland, has expressed his approbation, and we can do no less. I'm sure that when Spenser wrote those lines, centuries ago, he could never counted on them receiving such eloquent praise. 'I like that one'."

Beatrice laughed. The sound was harsh to Ned's ears; he started in his seat like a kicked dog, looking from Mrs Simpson to Beatrice and then back again.

"My husband, Theo, read all the great writers," Mrs Simpson told Ned, seemingly oblivious to his emotion. "I had read some of them before, of course, but after our marriage, he completed my education. We used to play a game, where he would start a quote and I would finish it. Now I have taught that game to Beatrice, and she has learnt it well, has she not?"

"Yes," Ned said, rearranging the position of his hands, where they rested on his knees. "Very well."

"Shall we try her out again?"

"I'm ready," declared Beatrice, and Mrs Simpson smiled in satisfaction.

What followed was a series of quotations, most of which Ned had never heard before, introduced by Mrs Simpson and completed by Beatrice. Sometimes Mrs Simpson would pass the game to him, but he could seldom think of a quotation in time, and would be forced to declaim, shaking his head. The one time he ventured, "'Ten thousand saw I at a glance...'", Beatrice swiftly answered, "'Tossing their heads in sprightly dance'... but really, what a common poem! Couldn't you think of anything better?"

Ned had always thought of himself as a pretty good reader; at least he was considered to be so back in Durham. Now his own ignorance crashed upon him, as he sat there, watching a game in which he could take no part, twitching and nodding his head every now and then like a marionette, wanting the floor to swallow him up.

At the first pause in the conversation, he judged it time to go, and announced his intention with a mumble, but Mrs

Simpson exclaimed, "Why, it hasn't even been half an hour! Are social calls in Durham usually this short?", and so he was obliged to sit there for another twenty minutes, until the entrance of Mr Morgan at last provided a distraction, and furnished the means for Ned, with a murmured farewell and a hasty bow, to make his escape. He exited the house with similar sensations as he had had on his last visit, that he should never like to come back here ever again, only this time, they came from a different source. Something that he had loved – with a different kind of feeling than the boyish ardour he felt for Beatrice, or the commonplace love he felt for his family – had just been taken from him, or at least, it had been held up before him and mocked until he did not feel it could be his own anymore.

Some tears must issue forth upon this loss; they had been held back in the presence of the ladies, but now they fell freely, as Ned blindly made his way to daylight. But he found himself in the overgrown garden rather than the front drive; in his confusion, unguided by the servant, he had taken the wrong way. He halted, feeling the grass blades tickle the space just above his ankles, which his trousers, that were slightly too short for him, left bare. The sun was dazzling his eyes, and his breath came in short, quick gasps. And even as he began to try to reason with himself – that his train home was in a few hours' time, that he'd better make no further delays and get on the road as soon as he could – he found that he could not move; he waited, seemingly in vain, for the racing of his heart to slow.

The sound of creaking door hinges behind him made Ned's hand jump to his face; he quickly dried his eyes, and half-turned in the direction of Beatrice. The glance of his eyes took in only an indistinct impression of her form: her dark hair and the plaid pattern of the dress that she was wearing. Then he began to move past her, towards the door through which she had just entered, as he said, in some confusion, "I was just... going..."

"Are you *crying*?" Her question stopped him in his tracks. "Because of our game? How silly!"

"I'm going now," Ned said again, without turning. Then, unable to help himself, he added, more firmly, "And I'm *never* coming back."

"But that's not true, is it?" With a swish of skirts, Beatrice had come level with him. "You mean to be a solicitor like your uncle when you're grown up, don't you? You'll have to come back to London to study how."

"I'll never be like him," said Ned, feeling a fury of embarrassment as his voice choked on the last word. "I don't ever want to come back here. I hate London – and I hate Frank Allen and Mrs Simpson and *you*..."

"I don't know who Frank Allen is. And you might very well hate Mrs Simpson – lots of people do." Beatrice stepped in front of Ned so that she was blocking his path. "But you don't hate *me*. You like me – very much, don't you? I can see it."

She was a little taller than him, and he fixed his gaze on the silver chain that hung around her white neck, the rest of it hidden under the folds of her dress.

"Not anymore," Ned managed to say.

"I don't believe you. You can't even look me in the eye when you say that." As Ned made another, involuntary motion with his hand, to dry his eyes again, she exclaimed, "You really *are* upset! And all over a little game? What a baby you are!"

"Leave me alone," said Ned, in a voice now thick with tears.

"Would you like to kiss me?" said Beatrice then. "I'll let you, to say sorry for making you cry."

"I don't –" Ned stopped short. Confusion and shock now adding to his agony, he didn't seem able to do or say anything; he was almost sure that Beatrice's offer was just another cruel joke. He stayed right where he was as Beatrice stepped forward, closing the distance between them. He held his breath as she put a hand to his shoulder and planted a kiss on his lips.

The sunlight made strange shapes and spots on the black of Ned's eyelids, which he had closed while Beatrice kissed him. "There," he heard her say as she stepped back again. "Now you won't think I'm so terrible."

Judging it safe to open his eyes, Ned did so, and found himself looking right into her own. This was a wonderful moment – or ought to have been. But there was something in the calm expression of Beatrice's eyes that made her look very like Mrs Simpson. Her eyes had not seen half so much as that lady's; surely they ought to look upon the world as though it were a fresh and happy place? Surely they oughtn't to look as Beatrice's looked now, as though – as though they had watched too many things die? In the flash of fear that passed through Ned upon that last thought, he reached protectively for Beatrice's hand, but she moved away from him before they could touch again. With a faint sound of laughter, and the swish of material, she had vanished again into the house.

Ned had just reached the bottom of the drive when he heard the sound of quick footsteps behind him. His first, thrilling thought was that it must be Beatrice, come after him to say a proper goodbye, as she had never done before – but, noticing an instant later that the steps were too heavy to be hers, Ned halted, and turned just as Mr Morgan reached him.

Before he knew what was happening, the man had grabbed him by the collar, the cheap fustian fabric tearing as he lifted Ned clear off the ground and thrust him up against the gate.

"I know what you're about!" Mr Morgan snarled, his face inches from Ned's own. "I know what game you're playing!"

"I'm not playing any –" Ned began, but was silenced as the man gave him a shake.

"You think now you've got some chance with her? Oh, yes, I saw you in the garden just now: I saw everything. But mark my words, she's laughing at you now, laughing and telling Mrs Simpson all about the fine trick she's played on you..."

"I'm sure she is," Ned said, his voice coming out funny as his collar dug into his throat.

"Don't play the fool with me! You know everything – you and Mr Perry both, and now you want to get the run on us. No doubt that was why he brought you down here in the first place, to introduce you to Mrs Simpson's heiress and put you in for thousands of pounds, maybe even the house too – but she'd never marry you..."

"I know she wouldn't," Ned choked.

"But you thought you'd try anyway? You thought to beat me to it? The girl is mine –" Mr Morgan gave Ned another shake, this one more violent than the last, "and I'll ruin her before I let another man marry her! She's mine, and always has been, from the moment Mrs Simpson brought her home – she's mine and always will be –"

The words died out in an indistinct snarl, but they had sent a chill through Ned, and even as he felt himself released, and lowered to the ground, he found he couldn't stand steady.

"I suppose I ought to thank you, really," Mr Morgan said, straightening his waistcoat while Ned stumbled and got a grip on the gate. "What we talked about before: it's quite clear to me now, how it's going to go. You've made it clear."

"That's good," said Ned, faintly, half-turned towards the gate. "Can I go now?"

He was let go, with the promise secured from him before he left that he would never come back – a promise that he had already given Beatrice, without really meaning it. Ned got back to the South Bank in time to get together his suitcase, and made it to his train with minutes to spare. His mother, welcoming him at the station in Durham, noticed right away the bruises around his neck. Having never been to London herself, she was quite ready to believe that its streets were full of dangers, and accepted without question his story of being mugged.

It was not until years later that Ned Hyland understood what Mr Morgan's last words had meant: that in the half-formed darkness of that man's mind, the gleam of gold was all that showed through, and that the kiss between Beatrice and Ned could not be explained otherwise. Mr Morgan had never loved someone unless he could gain some advantage from it, and imagining that Ned's mind must work the same way, he had taken the kiss as proof of what he had hoped: that Beatrice was indeed in for thousands of pounds, and perhaps the house, too, and that Ned Hyland, "tipped" by his uncle's professional knowledge, had been making his own bid for her.

3
COMING-OUT

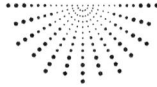

1 *855*

Beatrice Smith had learned many things from her guardian, including some very valuable lessons against indulging in sentimentality. There were some facts of life, as Mrs Simpson imparted to her, which could not be altered by any volume of tears cried: one of these facts was that people died, and the other was that a fool and his gold were soon parted. Mrs Simpson had accumulated quite a good deal of "gold", but luckily, as she explained to Beatrice, she was no fool and knew how to use it well. She had no intention of spreading it among various useless relations until it had lost all value.

"Only think," she told the young girl. "There are three different families who would have me believe that they all have an equal claim on me, after I die. If I were to listen – if I were to give them all I had, what do you think would happen?"

"You would have nothing left," Beatrice suggested.

"Exactly."

As far as Beatrice could see, there were only *two* families after Mrs Simpson's money: Mrs Simpson's extended family from before her first marriage, and the family of her most lately-deceased husband, Mr Simpson. Mr Morgan and Miss Simpson were only the most persistent members of these respective tribes; there were many others who had descended on the house in Highgate as soon as whispers of Mrs Simpson's illness reached them, and these others had been chased off in various ways. The Russells had never shown their faces at all. But Beatrice knew that it was better not to mention such things, because, while Mrs Simpson was perfectly happy to talk about her first husband, she did not like to be reminded of his family.

It had been 1849 when Mrs Simpson had first told Beatrice about her illness, though it was likely that she had known about it for even longer than that. A year later, through numerous conferences in the house in Highgate, she had written up her will with the help of the solicitor

Mr Perry, during which time Mr Perry's nephew from the North had come to visit London.

Beatrice had liked Ned, in so far as it was possible for her to really like anyone of his type. Ned was grubby and common and spoke with a funny accent, and meeting him had forced the realisation onto Beatrice's brain that not everyone was like her and Mrs Simpson – that, indeed, outside the walls of the house in Highgate, there was probably a whole country full of people who resembled Ned in many respects. Beatrice's memories of her time before Mrs Simpson were dim and shadowy; they belonged to a stranger, and all she had known since then were the people who populated Mrs Simpson's world. These people fell into two distinct categories: those who were directly employed by Mrs Simpson – servants and solicitors and doctors – and those who came in an informal capacity to provide some service for her, like Mr Morgan, who mended things around the house, and Miss Simpson, who provided "company" – in the hopes that they would be remembered in her will.

Beatrice's view of this latter category was reflective of Mrs Simpson's own. She had nothing but scorn for them. They were like mangy dogs, scrambling over the fence of the house in Highgate, gasping with their tongues hanging out, begging for a few scraps from their master. At least the servants and professionals understood that in order to get their wage, they must work; as such, Beatrice accorded them a distant respect, and placed Ned in the same category, since he was the nephew of Mr Perry.

But the Miss Simpsons and Mr Morgans of the world... Beatrice had learned from Mrs Simpson to laugh at them. She watched with amusement as they bustled about the house in Highgate, attempting to make themselves useful; she watched as the frenzied energy of their activities gradually died down, as one year turned into two, three, four, five, and still Mrs Simpson seemed perfectly healthy.

Her doctor was baffled. Given the nature of Mrs Simpson's illness, he had not counted on her surviving for so long. Watching her guardian's self-satisfied smile as she emerged from her latest conference with him, Beatrice wondered, privately, whether sheer force of will alone could keep a person alive. She had no doubt that Mrs Simpson's illness *did* exist: Beatrice had seen her, on occasion, laid up and feverish and too weak to get out of bed, but after each of these crises, her guardian had always rallied again. Each unexpected recovery dashed anew the eager hopes of her hangers-on. Beatrice, for her part, was glad to see their plans spoiled, and proud of Mrs Simpson for defying their expectations again – even if she was never quite sure how she managed to do it. Mrs Simpson, it sometimes seemed to Beatrice, was capable of controlling everything around her, even her own fate: she had pulled Beatrice out of darkness, after all, and ever since that long-ago day in the graveyard when they had first met, it would not have been a stretch to say that

Beatrice had attributed certain mystical qualities to the woman.

Beatrice owed everything to Mrs Simpson: the social world in which she moved was her guardian's, the name that she bore had been of her guardian's choosing, and even her birthday came from their first, fateful meeting in the graveyard. Since Beatrice could not remember the real date, or, as was more likely, it had never been told to her, they had taken to marking it on the anniversary of that day instead, which occurred around the same time as the anniversary of Mr Simpson's death. For the latter occasion, Mrs Simpson never stirred herself beyond wearing a black band around her sleeve; she had long since stopped wearing mourning or even half-mourning. But for Beatrice's birthday, she always made special efforts, and Beatrice's eighteenth birthday, being her official coming-out, merited the greatest efforts of all.

First of all, a new wardrobe was necessary: it was a point on which Mrs Simpson insisted and to which Beatrice could make no objections. There was no question of their going into town to purchase fabrics, since Mrs Simpson had not stepped over the threshold of the house in Highgate in ten years and did not intend to do so now. Instead, they spent days poring over catalogues and writing out orders. Miss Simpson, on another one of her extended visits from Dover, declared that they could not trust a servant to the task, and carried these orders herself to the post office. When the fabrics arrived, a fortnight later, she made herself useful in bearing them to Mrs Simpson's dressmaker, and carefully dictating to that faithful dressmaker the patterns which she had been shown by Beatrice and Mrs Simpson.

There were other preparations to be made, too. While Mrs Simpson had been resolute that to a host a ball would be beyond her capabilities, she had decided that a dinner party was necessary – that, to launch her long-term project, Beatrice, into society, she could do no less. As such, the house had to be cleaned from top to bottom, the formal dining-room aired and dusted, and several repairs undertaken. Since Mr Morgan was no longer at hand to offer his help in this domain, Miss Simpson busied herself overseeing these repairs instead, an interference which chiefly involved her ordering servants to do tasks that they had already started, and generally getting in everyone's way.

Mr Morgan, since last year, had been conspicuously absent from the house in Highgate, and though his absence had as good an explanation as was possible to be met with in those days – he had joined the army and was fighting for queen and country in Crimea – Mrs Simpson still seemed to take it as a personal slight. Beatrice, for her part, told herself that she didn't care. She had been taught by her guardian to contempt Mr Morgan, and everyone like him, and so she really believed that contempt was all she felt for him. Although as a younger girl she might have been dazzled by his good looks – which was natural enough since he was the only eligible man to be found around the house in Highgate, if you didn't count Mr Perry – she was sure that such fluttering, girlish feelings were past her now.

"Who is Edward Hyland?" asked Miss Simpson one day, when she was sorting through the invitations to check that no one had been forgotten, before the maid brought them to the post office.

"Oh, you remember," said Beatrice, turning this way and that as she regarded herself in the mirror. "Mr Perry's nephew, from the North. He came here once on a visit, a few years ago."

"I *do* remember a boy, rather rough-looking – and with funny manners." Miss Simpson put down the envelope and frowned at Beatrice. "But I'm sure no one expected you to invite *him*. Mr Perry, perhaps, but..."

"I know it wasn't expected," said Beatrice calmly. "I just thought it would be a nice thing to do for the poor boy. I can't imagine how dreadfully dull it must be to live somewhere like Durham. I'm sure he mustn't get many invitations to parties like this."

Miss Simpson's silence told her she was unconvinced. Mrs Simpson, meanwhile, seated close to the fire, had showed no signs thus far of attending to the conversation. Now, however, with a sly smile on her face, she said, "I think *I* know why Beatrice has invited him."

The other two turned to look at her, questioningly. "It's quite clear to me," Mrs Simpson continued. "She wants to add one more sacrifice to the flames. Isn't that so, Beatrice?"

Beatrice had enough shame left in her to blush, though she did not attempt to deny what her guardian had said. She turned back to regard her reflection. Her long-awaited wardrobe had finally arrived this morning, and all day, in consequence, she had felt that she was looking down at the world from a great height. As a girl, Beatrice had always dressed in old-fashioned styles, hand-me-downs from Mrs Simpson with thick sleeves and ankle-length skirts. Now that she was becoming a woman, it seemed only right that she should have the newest fashions, and Mrs Simpson, in putting herself to all this trouble and expense on Beatrice's behalf, had evidently agreed.

Beatrice was wearing now her favourite of the newly-arrived dresses: a white organdie with a voluminous, ruffled skirt that reached the floor. She ran a hand down one of the ruffles, listening intently as Mrs Simpson said, "Every young man who steps over the threshold of this house next Thursday night will fall in love with her. They would fall in love with her if she looked even half as beautiful as she does now. Wouldn't you agree, Eliza?"

"Oh yes," said Miss Simpson, with somewhat less enthusiasm. "She will certainly make a stir."

"And the poor boy, Ned Hyland, will be one of them," concluded Mrs Simpson. "I have no doubt of it."

"The poor boy, ma'am," said Beatrice, now feeling it necessary to defend herself, "is very lucky to have such an opportunity, is he not? And no one is forcing him to come. If he does, he will meet so very many interesting people here, connections that, I'm sure, if he still wishes to study law, will prove useful."

"Yes," agreed Mrs Simpson. "I have certainly invited a great many important people to your coming-out."

When Miss Simpson had brought the invitations downstairs to hand them to the maid, no doubt to issue very specific instructions on exactly how long it should take her to carry them to the post office and back, Mrs Simpson rose from her chair and made her way to Beatrice, until she was standing just behind her at the mirror. Her pale, curiously ageless face was reflected beside Beatrice's own, which was still flushed with pleasure and anticipation at the prospect of her power. No expressions gave Mrs Simpson away, as she scanned Beatrice from head to toe. Nonetheless, her amusement of a few minutes before seemed to have faded, if the words that she spoke next were anything to go by.

"You seem conscious of the opportunity that next Thursday will provide to our guests – the ease of making connections, the pleasure of seeing you. But what about the opportunity to yourself?"

Her guardian was silent for so long that Beatrice knew some reply must be expected. "I know it's important –" she began.

"You will have your pick of the men here," Mrs Simpson said. Now there was a hint of pride in her voice, as her reflected gaze met Beatrice's. "You need only wave your hand and collect them all around you. But you must choose well, as I did. You must choose someone who will give you consequence, and advance you. My Theo made me a thousand times better than I already was. I want only the same for you."

"Thank you, ma'am," said Beatrice after a moment. "I will... choose well."

There were some points in her guardian's speech that confused her, when she reflected on them later. Was Beatrice, after all, not *already* a person of consequence? Had Mrs Simpson not made her so, in adopting her thirteen years ago, in keeping her close by her side ever since and treating her as a daughter? But, Beatrice concluded after a time thinking over these points, it must be that Mrs Simpson only wanted to raise her even higher than she already stood: that, with her generous spirit, she would not be content until Beatrice, through marriage, had attained some queenly standing. Beatrice, in the fond fit of self-indulgence brought on by this conversation, really began to picture such a fate for herself, her imagination and vanity furiously working together, until she would not have been surprised to hear that royalty itself had been invited to her coming-out.

~

When Ned Hyland got the letter from London in the post, he had just come home from the mine. With his blackened hands, he could not pick up the piece of glossy white sheet of paper, penned in Beatrice's delicate hand and imbued with a fragrance that filled the kitchen. Instead he let his mother do the honours while he went to wash himself in the sink outside.

He came back in, shivering from his dousing in the cold water, to find his mother looking like the cat who had got the cream. "What does she say?" he asked, dropping into the seat across from his mother.

"She has invited you to her coming-out party, next Thursday," replied Mrs Hyland, passing the invitation across the table to Ned. He read it quickly, as though to confirm her words, and then put it aside and gave a laugh.

"Well! The witches' lair in Highgate, opened at last to the general public. I never would have guessed." Sensing the disapproving note in his mother's silence, Ned glanced up at her. "If you'd seen it, Mum, you'd know what I mean. It really is a queer place. All those curtains shutting out the daylight and no candles, except in the gallery where you're paraded past portrait after portrait of her dead's husband deader ancestors..."

"You've described it to me before," interrupted Mrs Hyland. "And it does sound a little peculiar – but isn't it kind of them to remember you?"

"It's another trick," said Ned, handing her back the invitation. "A joke of theirs. I told you how they liked to play jokes on me before, Mrs Simpson and Beatrice..."

"This Mrs Simpson seems like a strange woman," his mother conceded, "but Miss Smith is the one who wrote the invitation, after all, and if she really would, as she writes here, like 'the pleasure of your company' at her coming-out..."

"There's no chance," Ned interrupted. "Whatever you're thinking will happen, there's no chance on earth, so don't even –"

"... I think it would be a fine chance for you," his mother continued stubbornly, "even if you are only to be friends."

"There's no chance of that either," Ned sighed, and at his mother's questioning look, he shrugged his shoulders. "Probably she has only asked me out of obligation – probably only because Uncle Perry is going too."

"It's five years since you visited there," his mother pointed out.

"Aye, that's true," Ned said, "and five years since I've heard anything from them. So you see now why I might think this is a trick?"

He excused himself, before his mother could make any further arguments. The truth, which he only acknowledged to himself when in the privacy of his room, lying back on his iron bedstead, was that he had already made up his mind: he had made up his mind the moment that he had seen Beatrice's handwriting. She had asked him to be there, and he would accept, not because it was the 'fine chance' his mother described it to be; he had no such illusions. He simply had no choice in the matter, and the only thing really standing in the way of his going to London for a frivolous party was his father.

Ned's mother cleared away that obstacle that very same night. Mr Hyland got home from work later than his son – Ned, at sixteen, had not yet been trained in the heavy work of. the mines – and, after heating up his dinner for him, Mrs Hyland broke the news. Ned, sitting on his bed with a novel in hand that he was not making much headway with, heard snippets of the conversation from downstairs. "He didn't like it!" he heard his father's raised voice proclaim at one point, "He didn't like working for your brother, did he? So why go back?"

His mother said something about 'friends', to which Mr Hyland scoffed,

"Friends? Some friends these fine people are. You remember how they treated him – he told us."

Some time later, one of his mother's arguments broke upon Ned's ears. "You've had it your way, these past few years," she told his father. "And I haven't complained. If he's to be stuck down in that mine with you for the rest of his life, what harm can it do, now, for him to see a bit of the world?"

The argument died down not long after that. Ned finally put away his novel and leaned his head back on his pillow. Every muscle in his body ached from the day's work, and he knew that the next morning, before the light of dawn had broken across the sky, he and his father would have already left, summoned to work by that ghostly whistle in the darkness. With one hand, Ned traced the worn cover of the novel that lay on the pillow beside him. These days, he did not have much time or energy for reading. But since the arrival of Beatrice's invitation, a funny feeling had started to bubble in his stomach: the feeling that, after years of lying still, the pages in the novel of his life were beginning to turn again of their own accord, so quickly that he did not have the chance to read what was written on them.

≈

The day had come at last, the day that Beatrice knew would fix the course of the rest of her life. She spent its first moments in luxurious contemplation, her head propped by soft, downy pillows and turned slightly to the side as she surveyed, with pleasure, the corner of white material that was just visible around the door of her wardrobe. This would be her dress this evening: she had a childish impulse to change into it now and admire herself in the mirror. But the impulse was curbed at the sound of a knock, as her maid came in with Beatrice's breakfast.

Beatrice drank all her tea but ate only a corner of toast before sending the tray back: Mrs Simpson had advised her not to eat much of anything that day, so that once she was laced into her dress, she would not be subjected to any unpleasant, unladylike sensations. It was advice that Beatrice found easy enough to follow. In her excitement, it had been impossible for her to sleep well; likewise, it would have been impossible for her to keep down a meal.

She was amazed at the calm of everyone else around her, for the duration of that day. Could they not feel how every hour, every minute, was dragging along? Mrs Simpson's calm was not really surprising, since Beatrice had never seen *her* agitated, but that Miss Simpson, and the servants, and the Lewis cousins – they were from Mrs Simpson's father's side of the family, and had arrived in London early – could all be so mild and cheerful, as though this were just any other day, truly astonished Beatrice.

The conversation of these cousins – who were tradespeople – was mostly common and vulgar, revolving around market days and the prices of various things, and Beatrice did not pay much notice. But at one moment, she did hear some murmurings which caused her to sit up in her seat: that Mr Morgan, it seemed, was back in the country, and that he had made a good deal of money in the war.

They were sitting in the drawing room, with a few hours yet until the party was to start, and Beatrice, leaning towards her guardian, asked with every appearance of calm, "Do you think he will come?"

Mrs Simpson, who had not been attending to the conversation, blinked at her, and it was Miss Simpson who answered. "I'm sure he must be tired from his journey," she said. "I would be very surprised if he *did* come tonight – especially since we didn't think to send him an invitation."

Beatrice settled back into her seat in relief. It was not that she was frightened of meeting Mr Morgan; it was only that his presence, on such an auspicious day, would have made her a little confused and uncomfortable.

The moment came at last for her to change, and Beatrice, twirling around at her mirror, beheld herself as something close to angelic. The hushed praise of her maid confirmed this impression. Beatrice was then forced to stand still again while her maid pinned up those loose strands of dark hair that had come loose at the motion. But she did so very happily, her eyes following every minute change in her own complexion, how the subtle shifts in the evening light cast parts of her face into shadow, and made the flush of her cheeks all the more striking, the shine of her eyes all the brighter.

She came down to the drawing room to find, rather than the bevy of admirers that she had expected there, that no one had arrived yet except for Ned Hyland, and an old woman dressed in mourning crape. Beatrice didn't know who the old woman was, but she seemed to be such an important personage that even Mrs Simpson had ceded her usual place by the fire. Meanwhile, the Lewis cousins were tripping over each other trying to fetch the old woman a glass of wine, or a shawl to put around her knees, and only Ned Hyland and Miss Simpson stood apart.

Beatrice spared a single glance of acknowledgement for Ned, who seemed incapable even of forming a greeting, so awed was he by her appearance. Then she went straight to Miss Simpson, looking towards the old woman by the fire. "Who is she?" Miss Simpson, her lips pressed so tightly together that they had nearly disappeared, gave her no answer. Beatrice advanced across the room, her white skirts so light that she felt as though she was gliding rather than stepping. As she went, she drew the gaze of the Lewis cousins, some of whose faces took on the same, slightly dazed expression as poor Ned was wearing. The old woman was the last to look around. At close quarters, Beatrice could see that she must be around eighty, and had once been a fine-looking woman: she had dark colouring, hair that had gone silver instead of white, and deep-set blue eyes that gleamed in interest as they found Beatrice.

"Well," the old woman proclaimed after a moment. "She's pretty enough." Turning towards Mrs Simpson, who had taken an adjacent seat, "And she's not your daughter?"

"No," said Mrs Simpson. "She is not my daughter. She is my ward, Beatrice Smith. Beatrice, this is Mrs Honoria Russell, my mother-in-law."

Mrs Simpson had always taught Beatrice to guard her expressions when in company, but in that moment all her lessons failed her; Beatrice felt her jaw drop as she gazed at the old woman.

"I heard that a fine young lady was making her debut today," said the old woman, with a kindly air that instantly raised Beatrice's suspicions. "And I thought I'd come and wish you my best."

Uninvited, Beatrice added silently. So this was the mother of Theo, whom Beatrice had heard so much about! This was the woman whose mysterious falling-out with Mrs Simpson had made her averse even to the mention of her name from Beatrice's lips, and now she occupied a place of honour in Mrs Simpson's drawing room. One glance at her guardian, however, told Beatrice that this had not been her intention or plan. A flush had appeared on Mrs Simpson's face, the likes of which Beatrice had only ever seen during one of her feverish spells, and, deprived of her usual chair, she sat slightly forward in her new one, evidently ill at ease.

Upon this observation, the realisation followed, a moment later, that as this was *her* evening, and as Mrs Simpson so evidently was not herself, it fell to Beatrice to be mistress of the situation. She sank into a deep curtsy, and said as she rose, "You are very kind, ma'am. I hope you will stay for dinner."

"I hope there is room at the table!" rejoined Mrs Russell, seemingly evident on disquieting her, but Beatrice just smiled serenely and said,

"We will make sure of that." Then she summoned one of the servants and, by the door of the drawing room, issued new instructions about the seating arrangements. Coming back after the servant had departed, Beatrice noticed that Ned Hyland was still standing alone, and instead of rejoining Mrs Russell, who was, in any case, too occupied by the eager attentions of the Lewis cousins to continue their conversation, Beatrice entreated Ned to sit.

He did so reluctantly – and even more reluctantly agreed to take a glass of wine, his discomfiture only eased once Beatrice herself had done the same. She sipped her wine slowly, conscious of the fact that she had barely eaten all day, and feeling Ned's gaze on her all the time as they exchanged civilities. It was natural enough that he should be looking at her so much, especially since she had chosen to sit beside him – but Beatrice was surprised by how pleasant she found his fixed attention.

At the first interlude in their polite conversation, she remarked, "You have changed quite a bit, Mr Hyland."

He rejoined, in such a particular tone that she knew to take it as a compliment, "*You* haven't."

They began to talk about the last time they had met, and the changes that had come with the last five years. For Ned, at least, there seemed to have been many; he told Beatrice that he had begun to work in the mines like his father, but that his future was not yet settled. As he talked, Beatrice looked him over, as though to confirm her own earlier remark. His sense of fashion had unfortunately not improved with time; he was wearing the most awful brown suit. But his fair, curly hair, which had been shoulder-length and unruly then, was a bit shorter now and had clearly been carefully brushed. His jaw and shoulders were broader, and he was a few inches taller than Beatrice. But most significantly, his grey eyes had a new earnestness to them; it was more interesting to Beatrice than the look of stupefied admiration that they used to contain.

"Does your mother still want you to study law?" Beatrice asked, when Ned had finished giving his account of the mines.

"Yes –" he hesitated before going on, "But I'm not so sure I would like to."

"Would you prefer to work in the mines?"

"No," he said, with a rueful laugh. "I suppose I'm hoping to find something in between."

Ignoring this, as she ignored everything that she did not understand, Beatrice said, "You know, if you are still interested in studying law, there will be some interesting people at the party tonight. At dinner, I have taken care to seat you beside a Mr Lawrence, who is looking to hire a law writer. He has his own practice on Chancery Lane. You might find it more varied compared to your uncle's. By-the-by, I never received a reply to the invitation I sent him – will he be coming later?"

"He is a little under the weather," Ned replied, quietly. "So I have come on his behalf. And – of course – in answer to your kind invitation." He hesitated – he had been looking at his hands as he spoke, but now he glanced up at her in sudden decision. "You are very good, to have arranged things so that I might have interesting discussions tonight – but you should know that I have only come to see you."

Beatrice now judged it time to end their conversation, and made some excuse about talking to Mrs Russell and the Lewis cousins. Ned rose when she did, and Beatrice, wanting to show her gratitude for his honest declaration while at the same time not encouraging any repetitions in the future, placed a light hand on his forearm just for a few seconds. She felt him go very still as she did so. "I am very glad you came," she said, sincerely, and let go of him, moving into the crowd.

The drawing room grew warm as more and more guests crowded into it. The curtains, which had been left open for once, showed the window outside getting clouded up with condensation. No matter how crowded the room got, there was always a little space left around Beatrice, not just because of the sheer volume of her magnificent white skirts, but in a sort of silent tribute to her loveliness. She talked to so many people that she began to feel dizzy. She felt herself looked at so often, and so admiringly, that her former excitement completely died away until she found the whole thing quite tiresome.

Worst of all was when the time came to go down to dinner. What an undignified scramble there was then, as every man within a few feet of Beatrice tried to be the first one to take her arm! Several of the Lewis cousins made complete fools of themselves in the process, and a little way away she saw Ned Hyland hovering, with a hopeful look on his face. Beatrice was too annoyed by now to feel sorry for him, and as someone came up beside her and drew her arm through his, she turned, ready to resign herself to be escorted by whoever it was.

For a moment she was rendered speechless, as she looked up to meet an intense blue gaze; her eyes darted up to the black hair, cropped close to the scalp, and then down to the smooth, clean-shaven jaw, where a neat beard had been before: to the green evening coat and gleaming black boots. When at last she was capable of stammering out,

"Mr – Morgan…", she felt just as if she were a stupid, dazzled girl again. "I didn't see you arrive."

"No, of course you didn't," said Mr Morgan, tightening his grip on her arm as they walked towards the door of the drawing room, the crowd parting before them. "Too absorbed by your many admirers."

There was some quality simmering under that low voice – resentment, jealousy? Hearing it, Beatrice felt her heart begin to pound faster. "We were sure you would be too tired from your journey," she heard herself say, her voice coming to her own ears as though from a great distance.

"Oh, is that why I was not invited?" But here Mr Morgan turned a little towards her and smiled, so that she could see he was joking. Beatrice's fascinated eyes noted the flash of gold in his teeth, the darker tan of his skin, as though he had spent many hours under a hot sun. "Tired or not," he went on, "I wouldn't have missed this for the world."

Beatrice, feeling dizzier than ever by his words, was forced to clutch more tightly to his arm. They did not speak again until they were in the dining room, when the seating arrangements so carefully made by Beatrice forced them apart. She summoned one of the servants to fetch another chair and table setting for Mr Morgan, and he was crowded up between two Simpson relations at the other end of the table, as far away from her as it was possible to get. Yet all through the meal, Beatrice felt his blue gaze like a magnetic force; every time she looked in his direction, she would find *him* looking at *her*.

She stopped attending to the general conversation, completely neglecting the important role of hostess that she had assigned herself earlier. She did not know whether the Lewises were happy with their positions, whether Miss Simpson was grateful to have been seated away from Mrs Russell, or whether Ned and Mr Lawrence did indeed get talking about law, as she had intended. Beatrice only remembered one snatch of conversation reaching her ears during the course of that meal: it struck her in particular because it was so strange.

"I'm grateful," she heard Mrs Russell saying, "We are all grateful –" And then Mrs Simpson, who was seated to Mrs Russell's right and Beatrice's left, said, in a curt, embarrassed tone that Beatrice had never heard before,

"We don't need to speak of it."

But Beatrice overheard no more pertinent remarks after that, since Mrs Russell turned away to talk to her other neighbour, and Mrs Simpson subsided into her usual placid silence.

With every new course that was presented before her, Beatrice's mouth watered, but she was careful not to take more than a few bites of anything. Once, when she was enjoying her pudding a little too much, she sensed Mrs Simpson's disapproving gaze and quickly put down her spoon, the feeling of hot shame that flooded through her more than sufficient to ruin her appetite. Likewise, she only took tiny sips of her wine, and as the other glasses at the table emptied and filled up again, hers remained untouched.

After dinner, rather than retreating back to the drawing room, the ladies made for the formal parlour at the front of the house instead. It was necessary to pass through the gallery in order to do so, and Beatrice shivered as she walked, the flimsy wrap around her shoulders only providing the barest protection from the cold of the winter's evening. In the parlour, a card-table had been set up, and some of the older ladies began to play whist, while the younger ladies formed a little cluster and began to talk about the latest plays and concerts of the season. They made no opening for Beatrice, and Beatrice, likewise, gave them no encouragement. She had seen, at a glance towards the group, that, while some were pretty, none of them were in danger of matching her radiance, and that was all that concerned her.

Even before dinner, she had already begun to feel that the evening would be a disappointment; now the full anti-climax of it broke upon her. Here she was, sitting awkward and alone at her own party! She had had such visions – such silly visions of all the wonderful, surprising things that might happen... and what had surprised her, in the end, apart from the presence of Mrs Russell and Mr Morgan escorting her down to dinner? *Mr Morgan...* Beatrice's thoughts latched on him now, as she thought again of his low, thrilling tone of voice, of how he had looked at her during dinner.

Before she knew it, she was out of her seat and murmuring her excuses to the ladies about fetching something warmer to put around her shoulders. Mrs Simpson made no objection, but of *course* Miss Simpson had to interfere, springing up from the card table to follow Beatrice to the door. "But you must let me go for you, my dear," she insisted. "This is your night! Stay right here and I will go to your room to find something – I do not mind in the least, if you will only tell me what I am to look for. A shawl, or a cloak, or cape..."

Beatrice, who had never been very patient with Miss Simpson to begin with, was in no humour to deal with her now. One hand on the door, she made a careless half-turn towards the other woman. "Just this once, Eliza Simpson, if you would *not mind* staying out of other people's affairs, I would be very grateful."

She had spoken low, but not low enough to avoid some of the young ladies nearby overhearing: a few nervous titters greeted Beatrice's words, and Miss Simpson flushed darkly. Smiling to show that she was unrepentant, Beatrice passed out of the parlour and down the gallery once more, hurrying now and clutching her wrap more tightly around her shoulders. But instead of turning for the stairs, she halted near the door of the dining room, listening for a moment to the sound of the men's voices within. The door stood ajar, and as Beatrice watched, it pushed open: a skein of blue smoke escaped, and was followed closely by Mr Morgan, who adjusted the pipe in his mouth when he saw her. His gaze swept her from head to toe, and, with a quick but discreet gesture, he closed the door of the dining room behind him.

"You know what you look like, standing there," he said, in that same low voice that he had used earlier, which seemed intended only for her ears. "In the half-light, with your dark hair and that expression on your face: you look like a siren. And your dress is just like sea foam."

"That is a very pretty compliment," Beatrice said, taking a step back, "thank you. I was just about to go upstairs to fetch something warm to..."

"Don't lie. You came to look for me, didn't you?" Mr Morgan put his pipe to his lips, taking a puff as he waited for her answer, while Beatrice, unsure herself of what the answer was, could only stare at him like a startled fish.

"I – I don't –"

Mr Morgan put his pipe on an end table, and came forward, reaching out a hand and taking Beatrice's in his before she had time to argue. "Come," he said, and led her away from the dining room.

∽

The night that had, thus far, proved disappointing for Beatrice had been even worse for the most earnest of her admirers. Ned, of course, in coming to London, had had no expectations of success. As it turned out, there was no cruel reversal awaiting him; the invitation *had* been genuine this time, and both Beatrice and Mrs Simpson had greeted him upon his arrival as though his presence there was perfectly natural. The cruelty came later: it came in the thrill of joy that rippled across his skin when he first saw Beatrice; it came in the leap of his heart when she came to sit beside him, and then the throbbing of his pulse as she stayed, and talked, and fixed her eyes upon him as though he were interesting to look at. Ned didn't think that his pounding heart slowed down a fraction of a beat in the fifteen minutes or so that they sat together. He would have felt frightened for himself if he hadn't felt so happy.

For a while after that, he was sure of everything. He was sure that he would get to escort her down to dinner – and then, when Mr Morgan showed up to perform that duty instead, sure that Beatrice would contempt him as she should. She was a grown woman now, even more beautiful than she had been as a girl, while Mr Morgan was still the grubby, grasping hanger-on that he had always been. Ned could see it plain enough, that under his gold teeth and fine clothes, Morgan was still desperate for Mrs Simpson's attention. He watched the man carefully during dinner, and noted that his gaze strayed more often in the direction of Mrs Simpson than anyone else.

But then there was Beatrice seated beside Mrs Simpson, and the frequent glances that passed between Mr Morgan and *her*, which Ned could not ignore. He kept waiting for her eyes to find him instead, to give some acknowledgement of their earlier conversation, and some promise that it might be continued later. But Beatrice did not look at Ned once. By pudding, he was so sunk in his own misery that he barely attended to his neighbour Mr Lawrence's questions, and couldn't remember how he answered them.

You should know that I have only come to see you, he had said to Beatrice earlier, after she had advised him to take the opportunity to talk to Mr Lawrence. Had he really been so brazen – so stupid as to think that a confession like that would be well-received – that after five years, she had thought of him even *half* so often as he had thought of her? He was lucky she hadn't laughed in his face.

When the ladies had retired, that white blur at the edge of Ned's vision – for he could not bear to look at Beatrice anymore – passing out of the dining room last of all, Ned turned from contemplating his own misery to watching his rival, Mr Morgan. As the men moved around the table, readjusting their positions and passing around a bottle of port, Ned saw how Morgan stayed at the edge of things. Puffing away on his pipe, he evidently had no interest in any of the men present, not seeming to notice or care that the boy he had once threatened for kissing Beatrice sat right across from him. Watching as

Morgan's long, ringed fingers tapped on the table, Ned realised that he must be waiting for something – waiting for –

"Ned Hyland! I've been trying to catch your eye for the past two hours."

A very friendly young man had just stopped by Ned's chair and was forcing him to shake hands. As Ned did so, he peered up at him uncomprehendingly. The man had a shock of black hair, a smattering of freckles over his nose, and was grinning from ear to ear. Ned was sure that he had never seen him before – and yet, as the man dropped into the seat beside Ned with a familiar movement, half-awkward, half-languid, Ned was suddenly brought back to his uncle's office. "Frank Allen!"

"You didn't recognise me? Maybe it's these," said Frank, running his hand along his sideburns, but Ned knew it wasn't that: it was because he didn't remember ever seeing the other boy smiling before.

"How's old Perry?" Frank asked, passing Ned the bottle of port and then, as Ned made no movement, pouring it into his glass for him. "Not here tonight, I notice?"

Ned gave Frank the same explanation that he had given Beatrice, and Frank frowned as he listened. "Under the weather, is he? Overworked?"

"I think so." Ned hesitated, and then, with a faint smile, "His new clerk isn't much good."

"Ha! Glad to hear I'm a little missed. But really, that man should get out of his office once in a while. Breathe some fresh air, take in some sights of the country. You know I travel a good deal now, for my work? Only around merry old England, of course, but I can tell you there's still plenty to see even in small towns."

"I'd say," said Ned, and Frank, encouraged, began to talk for a while about his new job, which, as Ned gathered, was as a journalist for some workers' paper based in London. He was only half-listening; his attention, while Frank talked, was on Mr Morgan, who had now risen from the table and was prowling around the perimeter of the dining room like a hunting cat. As Ned watched, Morgan reached the door of the dining room, took a puff on his pipe before stepping out, and shut the door behind him. He did so very quietly, so that the hinges barely made a sound, but Ned flinched all the same.

" – Hyland?" Frank had stopped talking, and Ned jerked back towards him, mumbling an apology.

"So, as I was saying, we're trying to get a picture of what's going on around the country, with the factory strikes in Blackburn and Preston and now talk of the miners in Northumberland coming out in support..."

"Yes," said Ned, lifting his glass of port to his lips and trying not to let his hand shake.

"... and we'd be glad of your point of view, being from

Durham. Well, you've spent some time in the mines by now, I gather?"

"Yes."

"Any sign of a strike there?"

"In Durham?" Ned said, in some alarm. "No, no."

"But discontent over wages, maybe, or the long hours?" Finally seeming to catch on that Ned was distracted, Frank gave up. "Anyway, we can talk about it another time. Are you staying in London for a few days?"

"Yes, at least. Since my uncle isn't well, I want to stay and see what I can do for him."

"Poor old Perry," said Frank, sighing. "Well, how about tomorrow, then? I could drop over to the office, get a look at this new clerk too."

"All right."

"Fine." Frank clapped him on the shoulder as he rose from the table. "I'd better go mingle a bit. I'm sure most of the people Mrs Simpson has invited wouldn't be the sort to read my paper, but then again, you never know." He lingered for a moment more, though, and said, in an undertone, "She certainly looked the part tonight, didn't she? Our Miss Smith."

"She certainly did," was all the response Ned could manage to that, and for the rest of the evening, because he knew by now that Beatrice did not really see him, he did not really see *her*, either. Sitting in the parlour, while people played cards and conversation buzzed around him, he kept watching the clock. It had been a fine chance, his coming here, and now that he had squandered that, all he was waiting for was his chance to go home. His mind was already back in Durham, even though, as he had told Frank, he knew that he would be stuck in London for the next few days.

~

"Are you going to lure me to my distress, Beatrice?" said Mr Morgan. He had led her by the hand out to the garden, and, when she had complained of the cold, put his own evening coat around her shoulders.

"I – don't know," said Beatrice, too distracted by the fact that he had used her first name, and by the feeling of soft wool against her bare arms, to puzzle out what he meant.

"Like the sirens in the stories," Mr Morgan pursued, tracing a pattern on the skin of her palm. Then he paused. "Where are your gloves?"

"They're inside," Beatrice said, half-turning towards the door. "I should go fetch them...."

"No, I like you like this. Stay just where you are." He had both of her hands in his now, and Beatrice, who had gone still at his command, allowed him to draw her in a little closer. He smelled of smoke and salt and spice, of danger and wild seas and exotic lands... she looked up at him, feeling dizzy.

"You ignored me all through dinner," Mr Morgan said quietly. "And I haven't seen you these past two years. A man's patience has its limits, you know, Beatrice."

That sense of danger was growing with every word that came out of his mouth. "I wasn't aware that our parting had been a source of pain to you," she managed to say, but he only tugged her closer, a little more forcefully than before.

"Don't try those coquettish tricks on me. You know very well that it's only ever been you, for me. You know very well that I've only been waiting for you to get old enough until we can be married."

"Married?" Beatrice repeated. "I had no idea – and I have no intention –"

"'No intention?' Wasn't that what tonight was all about, to parade you in front of your suitors and see who made a bid for you? Well, your trick worked – or perhaps it was Mrs Simpson's trick. It worked only too well." Here Mr Morgan let go of her hands, and cupped her face with his hands.

Beatrice now had the sense that something dreadful was about to happen. "Oh, no –" she breathed, just seconds before Mr Morgan pulled her in and crushed the sound from her lips with his kiss.

His passion had not been mere words; she felt it now in the way that he kissed her, as his hands moved from her face to her waist, clutching her ever closer. Perhaps that was why she let it all go on for much longer than she should have. When she finally managed to break away, breathless, it was just in time to see a pale, startled face retreating into the house, and a gloved hand closing the door behind them.

"Oh, no," Beatrice breathed again, and then turned the full force of her dismay and anger on Mr Morgan. "I think that was Miss Simpson! Oh, why did you have to do that *here, now?*"

"I couldn't help it," said Mr Morgan, smiling as though it was all a great joke. "I don't see how any man could have helped it. Besides, what do you care what Eliza Simpson thinks?"

"I don't, of course, but it just seems..." Beatrice shook her head, trying to get her thoughts straight. Holding out her hands to keep Mr Morgan at bay, for he was advancing towards her again. "No, you mustn't –"

He kissed her for a second time, with such force that his coat slipped from her shoulders. Enclosed in his arms, however, Beatrice did not feel the cold as much as she might otherwise have done, and, once again, she allowed the kiss to go on for much longer than she should have. Finally pulling away, she gasped, "I must go back. They'll be wondering..."

"Very well," said Mr Morgan, smiling down at her, and Beatrice detached herself from his arms, hurrying back into the house. She clutched her wrap around her shoulders as she went, unsure how she was going to face everyone in the drawing room as though nothing had happened. She had had no idea that it was possible to feel as many emotions as she seemed to have discovered that evening: anger and excitement and joy and fear and shame, all competing for their place.

4

TWO SUITORS

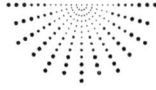

This riot of new sensations within Beatrice had settled, by the next morning, into a steady glow of contentment. She stretched luxuriously on her pillows and smiled up at the ceiling, secure in the knowledge that Mr Morgan loved her, confident that he must be thinking of her then and there. She took her time dressing, pausing every now and then to relive a certain moment or other from the night before: the look of awe on everyone's faces when she had first entered the drawing room in her finery; the earnest devotion in Ned Hyland's eyes as he had spoken to her, or the barely restrained passion in Mr Morgan's voice as he had all but proposed to her in the garden: the force and surety with which he had taken her in his arms, and claimed her first kiss (Beatrice did not count the kiss with Ned Hyland, five years before, and had almost forgotten it entirely).

It seemed unfair to go back to one of her drab day-dresses after shining in such brilliance all night. But Beatrice's mind was already working forward, towards her next social appearance, whenever that would be: she began to plan out what she would wear, picturing the stir that she would make. Perhaps the theatre, or some private party: she might wear that new green silk, which would look very well with her dark hair. Mrs Simpson would not be able to come, of course, since she never left the house, but she could advise Beatrice beforehand on all the important personages that she was to meet, and the impression that she ought to make...

Beatrice would gladly have spent her whole morning in such pleasant daydreams, but while she was taking her breakfast, the butler came in and advised her that Mrs Simpson was having breakfast in bed.

"Oh, I hope she's feeling well," said Beatrice, her fork pausing in mid-air.

"Yes, Miss Smith, just a little over-tired from last night's exertions, I would say."

"Of course. Tell her I'll be up to see her as soon as I've finished eating."

"If you please, miss..." The butler hesitated, and Beatrice looked up at him curiously.

"Yes, Armstrong?"

"Well, she has asked that you come to see her now. Without delay."

It was a moment before Beatrice could take this in. She was very hungry, having eaten almost nothing the previous day. With a wistful glance at her poached eggs – and the toast piled at the corner of her plate that she had barely touched – she wiped her hands on her napkin and got to her feet.

She found Mrs Simpson sitting up in bed, enjoying a similar repast to the one that Beatrice had just abandoned downstairs, though Mrs Simpson's toast was dry, as was recommended for invalids, and in place of coffee, she had cocoa.

"I am so glad to see that you have an appetite, ma'am," Beatrice said eagerly, as soon as she had pulled up a chair by Mrs Simpson's bedside. "I was worried, when Armstrong told me you were still in bed, that you might have had a relapse. After all your exertions last night..."

"Yes, indeed," Mrs Simpson said, once Beatrice had trailed off, fixing her ward with those calm, impenetrable eyes. "Of which there were more than you can even imagine. I had no idea, for instance, that Honoria Russell would feel it her duty to show up and pay her respects to you. *That* took me by surprise, I will admit."

"Yes, it was so very strange," Beatrice agreed, casting her own mind back over the events of the night, which, admittedly, following her encounter with Mr Morgan in the garden, became rather fuzzy. "But I believe she left earlier than the rest?"

"She did," confirmed Mrs Simpson. "Not long after dinner." She took another sip of her cocoa and said, with her eyes still on Beatrice, "Eliza has been to see me this morning."

"Eliza Simpson?" Beatrice said, barely managing to keep her voice steady, as once again, her recollection bore her back to that moment in the garden last night – but this time with fear instead of pleasure, as in her mind's eye, she saw that pale, startled face disappearing behind the door.

"Yes, I know no other Elizas, do you?"

"I was just – surprised," Beatrice defended herself against her guardian's sarcasm, "that she didn't stop to bid me good morning."

"You won't be so surprised when you hear what she had to say. She is most shocked at your behaviour last night, and disappointed in you. She tells me that you were in the garden for some time, allowing James Morgan to take liberties with you, when you should have been attending your own party..."

Mrs Simpson's calm, neutral voice had not altered in its cadence, but Beatrice felt the dark flush creeping up her neck to her face. "I didn't –"

"Do you deny it?"

"No," said Beatrice, miserably.

"Then you did allow my cousin to take liberties with you?"

"Yes – but I asked him not to. I told him we shouldn't – I knew it would look badly if anyone saw... but he was so insistent; he said he's always loved me since I was a girl, that he wants to marry me –"

"I daresay he does," Mrs Simpson said, pursing her lips. "And – so? You were flattered into allowing his advances, against your own better judgement?"

"I think so." Beatrice nodded, and fixed her eyes on her guardian in wide appeal. "Oh, please try to understand. I didn't mean for it to go that way. It was all just so exciting, his being back after so long abroad, and the way he looked, and the things he said..."

"You shouldn't have followed him out to the garden in the first place, if you knew there was a danger that you might get carried away by his attentions."

"I know. I wasn't thinking..."

"But I do understand, you know." Beatrice, who had hung her head for a second time, lifted it again in relief at the sound of her guardian's words. "I had many suitors when I first came out, too. And there were times when I might myself have gotten carried away – when I might have ruined my chances with Theo – but girls were more strictly chaperoned back then." Mrs Simpson sighed. "It's one thing we have lost, these days. And I must admit some of the blame myself. I have always let you do as you please: I didn't see the use in imposing any rules on you. But maybe one or two rules might not have gone amiss..."

There was something new in Mrs Simpson's voice, a note of finality, which made Beatrice's mouth go dry. "What..." she began, but her guardian interrupted,

"*I* might understand why you let things slip last night, Beatrice. I was young and beautiful and vain myself once, too." Beatrice's flush deepened as she heard the last adjective, which had never before escaped Mrs Simpson's lips in reference to her. "But Eliza Simpson has been plain her whole life, and you see, Beatrice, it is *so* much easier for plain people to be good. She can't understand how you let temptation get the better of you. And, unfortunately, after what she witnessed last night, she felt it her duty not only to tell the Lewises about it, but my brothers and sisters-in-law, too, as well as the rest of her acquaintances in town, which, as I'm sure you can guess, means that the story will be all over London by this evening. *Beatrice.*"

Her ward had sprung to her feet, causing the legs of her chair to scrape along the floor. "This has nothing to do with *duty*," Beatrice said, bitterly. "This is Eliza getting her own back – for the way I spoke to her."

"How did you speak to her?"

"The same way I always do – well, perhaps a little worse." Beatrice quickly related what she had said to Eliza in the drawing room, before she had gone out to the garden.

Mrs Simpson's expression did not change as she listened, but she sighed again once Beatrice had concluded her account.

"And you say that the other young ladies heard it, too? She must have been embarrassed, and angry. No wonder she felt no obligation to discretion, once she had seen you with James in the garden. Beatrice..."

"What?" Beatrice was moving for the door.

"There is nothing you can do. Eliza Simpson has a very busy morning ahead of her. She will be visiting the house of everyone she knows in London, to relate the story. And after that, once she goes back to Dover, she will no doubt continue to talk of it..."

"Couldn't you have stopped her?" Beatrice exclaimed. She didn't remember ever feeling unnerved before at Mrs Simpson's eternally calm demeanour, but now it positively flummoxed her. "When she came this morning, to warn you about what she had seen? She might have told some people already, but you could at least have stopped it from getting worse..."

"She didn't come here to warn me, Beatrice," Mrs Simpson said. "She came here to gloat, about what she has already achieved. She is almost as angry at me as she is at you – she thought I had invited Honoria Russell here, and took it as a slight, after I didn't invite old Mrs Simpson – who is over eighty and half-blind, and certainly wouldn't have *wanted* an invitation to a young girl's coming-out..."

"Tell me," Beatrice pleaded, coming forward again. "Tell me what this means. Surely a rumour like this – will blow over, in time? Maybe, if we delay my coming-out by a few months –"

"Beatrice," said Mrs Simpson, almost gently. "There's to be no coming-out now. We can't draw any more attention to you."

Beatrice's legs buckled beneath her, and within seconds, she found herself kneeling by her guardian's bedside. "But..." she said numbly. "But I was so looking forward to it all."

"I know you were."

They were both silent for a minute or two. Mrs Simpson's gaze strayed past Beatrice, and her eyes took on that familiar, distant look: Beatrice knew that it meant she was thinking of her past, and that soon her own plight would have slipped her guardian's mind. To bring Mrs Simpson's attention back to herself before that happened, she forced herself to speak. "So – if I'm not to come out then I can't marry, can I?"

Mrs Simpson blinked, and looked at Beatrice incredulously for a moment. "Oh no," she said, at length. "No, you must marry. It's the only thing to be done now: the only thing that will save your reputation. You must marry James."

~

Ned was not particularly surprised by the piece of news that Frank Allen carried to Mr Perry's office the day after the party, though the other young man had evidently expected him to be. "It's quite something, isn't it?" Frank said, eagerly. "All that to-do about her coming-out – and then they find her carrying on with that Morgan fellow. The old lady must be hopping mad."

Ned glanced back at Mr Perry's spotty-faced clerk, Collins, who was showing rather too lively an interest in their conversation even though he was supposed to be copying out letters – Mr Perry himself still being confined to bed. "Let's talk about this somewhere else."

"All right, then," Frank said, watching as Ned took up his cap and scarf, "but not outside, if you please. My toes are still half-frozen from the walk here." All the same, he followed Ned downstairs obligingly enough, stooping to avoid hitting his head on the sloped ceiling, and only showed his relief by a small sigh when, instead of directing them out the street door, Ned directed them left instead.

Mr Perry's housekeeper, Miss Pleasant, kept a small parlour of her own on the ground floor of the office building, and was happy enough to allow the two young men use of it for half an hour, provided that they listened to her chatter as she set about stoking the fire. Once she was satisfied that they would be warm enough, and had pulled the door of the parlour behind her, Frank blew out his breath. "Well, I thought she'd never go. Anyway, so

Morgan and Miss Smith were seen in the garden in a rather interesting position –"

"He must have forced her," Ned said at once.

"Forced her?" Frank gave a wry smile. "From what I hear – from the looks of it – she wasn't being forced into anything..." He stopped short, the smile fading from his face at the look Ned gave him. Clearing his throat, "Well, maybe you're right –"

"He tricked her, or confused her somehow," Ned insisted. "I was watching him, while you were talking to me after dinner. I could see that he was planning something."

"I remember you told me once," Frank said, looking thoughtful, "that you thought she liked him. That she might marry him one day."

"Maybe she did like him, back then. Maybe she still does." Ned could feel his own face warming, and it wasn't from the heat of the fire. "But she *can't* marry him. He's only interested in her money – in Mrs Simpson's money. He said to me before..." He stopped short.

"What? What did he say?" The chair that Frank had chosen was so small as to make him look rather comical in it: his long arms almost reached his calves as he leaned forward in his eagerness.

Ned hesitated, and then related the story of Beatrice kissing him, and how Mr Morgan had seen them together and threatened him afterwards. "He said... that he'd rather ruin her than let someone else have her."

Frank gave a low whistle. "Well, now it looks like he's done exactly what he said he would. He's ruined her, so no one else will want her. She'll *have* to marry him."

"She *can't* marry him," Ned repeated, "And anyway, why should she be ruined just for a stupid kiss? In Durham..."

"We're not in Durham," Frank said, "We're in London. We – where are you going?"

Ned had gotten to his feet. "I'm going to Highgate."

"Now?"

"I've got to talk to Mrs Simpson. I've got to tell her everything I know about Morgan. Once I tell her, there's no way she can force Beatrice to do this. Beatrice should be free to marry whoever she wants – she shouldn't be punished for one mistake." Ned caught his breath, and, seeing the doubt on Frank's face as he looked up at him, pressed on before his friend could interrupt, "Will you tell my uncle where I've gone? I don't know how long I'll be."

"I'll tell him," Frank said, turning in his small chair to watch Ned go, "but, you know, I *was* hoping to get a chance to talk to you about the paper..."

"That'll have to wait," Ned said over his shoulder, and pulled the door behind him. He stepped out the street door into the raw wind, hesitated, and then turned left.

With one hand pressed on his cap to keep it from blowing away, he made for the river. His other hand pressed his coat pocket, to find a few shillings there. A cab to Highgate might cost him a quarter of his wages for a week, but he had no time to lose.

~

Not long after Beatrice's conversation with Mrs Simpson that morning, Mr Morgan arrived, evidently having been summoned by a note. He spent some time shut up with Mrs Simpson in her room. Beatrice, who had only glimpsed him from an upstairs window, striding into the house as though he had nothing to be ashamed of, hoped that she would not have to face him yet. To relieve her feelings, she found her old sketchbook and tore up all the drawings that she had made of Mr Morgan years ago. Then she banged about a bit on the piano, and finally gave up, resting her head on the piano keys.

At the sound of the door opening, she did not raise her head. If it was Mrs Simpson, she reasoned, they had said all that could be said already. If it was a servant, she knew that they would take the hint and go away. And if it was Mr Morgan...

"You and I seem to be in quite a bit of trouble," came a low, familiar male voice, and Beatrice stiffened but still did not change her position. She heard his footsteps, soft and slow over the carpet. He was not in a hurry like last night, but taking his time, sounding her out. At last she sensed him pause a few feet from her. "Well? Beatrice?"

"I don't want to talk to you," she said to the piano keys.

"I'm sure you don't. And I did behave quite badly last night, I will admit. If I had known that Eliza Simpson would go telling the whole world what she had seen, I'm sure I would have tried harder not to kiss you. But can you blame me, Beatrice? The way you looked..."

Despite herself, Beatrice felt her breath catch. She hoped that he hadn't heard – but when he took her hand a moment later, enclosing it in both of his, she knew that he must have.

"You look more human today," he said, musingly. "More a creature of the earth..."

"Let go of me," Beatrice said.

"I will, if you say it like you mean it." Beatrice was silent. She heard the smile in Mr Morgan's voice as he said next, "Well, then. Are you really going to worry about what an old spinster thinks of you? What business is it of Eliza Simpson's if we want to be happy together?" His grip tightened on her hand. "Beatrice. Don't you want to be happy with me?" She drew in another deep breath. "I can feel that you do."

He freed one of his own hands to touch her hair, moving his fingers lightly over the nape of her neck. Beatrice did not move a muscle, and a moment later, he let go of her again. She heard him stoop and bend until he was kneeling beside the piano stool. Warily, she lifted her head, and felt his hand on her arm, gently tugging her around until she was facing him.

"There, now," said Mr Morgan, smiling up at her as he took her hand again. "This isn't so bad, is it? You and I can be married as soon as you like. And we needn't invite any of those horrid people from last night – we needn't even invite Mrs Simpson, if you don't want to."

"No," Beatrice murmured, "She should be there."

"If you wish it, my darling." Mr Morgan reached up and cupped her cheek with his hand. "Now, don't look so worried. Show me one of those radiant smiles you were giving out so carelessly last night." He waited, and when she didn't oblige, sighed. "Well, if you won't smile at me, I suppose I shall just have to make you smile." He raised himself up on his knees, and as Beatrice shrank back instinctively, caught hold of her again. "What is it?"

"This is what started all the trouble," Beatrice reminded him.

"But what harm can it do now?" One hand on her shoulder, keeping her in place, Mr Morgan leaned forward and kissed her. Breaking away a minute later, he said, "There. Has the world fallen to pieces?"

Beatrice shook her head, and he rose to his feet, tugging her up with him until they were both upright. He looked like he was getting ready to kiss her again when something fluttered under his foot. "What's this?" Looking down, Mr Morgan stooped and picked up the torn piece of paper. Before Beatrice could snatch it out of his hand, he had flattened it out against the side of the piano. "Is this one of your old sketches of me? And you tore it up?" He began to laugh. "Goodness, it seems you really *were* upset."

"I'm *still* upset," Beatrice insisted. "And it's no laughing matter. My reputation..."

"Balderdash. Who cares about a reputation when you can be happy with me?" Mr Morgan put a careless arm around her shoulders and pulled her against his side, still looking at the sketch. He started to laugh again, and they were standing so close now that she could feel the movement of his muscles. "I can tell that life with you is going to be interesting, Beatrice Smith."

"You must let go of me," Beatrice told him again, managing to sound stern. "We must act properly until we are married."

"Until we are married. Yes, my darling, you're quite right." Still, Mr Morgan seemed in no hurry to let go of her, and as Beatrice began to detach herself, he leaned in to whisper in her ear, "I shall be counting every minute until then."

～

It was raining when the cab brought Ned up to the house in Highgate, and since he didn't feel like standing at the gate for ten minutes with water sluicing down his neck, he didn't bother ringing the bell. He just climbed the gate, splashing his trousers with mud as he landed hard on the other side. He didn't care how he looked or came across, all of his being now animated with one purpose. Up the drive he strode, glaring at the windows of the house and feeling that they almost glared back.

The butler who answered the door frowned at him. "Did you ring?"

"I've come to see Mrs Simpson," Ned said by way of response. "I need to speak with her, now."

"Mrs Simpson is in bed. She is not receiving visitors..."

"I'm here on behalf of my uncle," Ned interrupted. "Mr Perry. It's a matter concerning her will."

The butler's expression changed. "Very well. In that case, you'd better come in."

Ned, whose heart was pounding with the lie he had just told, followed the servant inside and allowed himself to be divested of his wet things. He walked after him down the dusty gallery, up the creaky stairs, and then up again, to a part of the house that Ned had never seen before. They passed an open door and Ned, with an involuntary glance inside, saw a white dress hanging in the door of a wardrobe: the white dress that Beatrice had been wearing last night. His heart began to beat even faster as he realised that this must be her room – something of her fragrance even seemed to linger on the air – but then he was forced to follow on after the butler, who stopped a few more doors down.

The butler began to knock, softly and discreetly. "She may be asleep," he said over his shoulder to Ned, and Ned half-closed his eyes: this was a possibility that he had not even considered, and what an anti-climax to his efforts it would be!

But at length, a faint voice sounded through the door, and the butler stepped in, leaving it ajar. Ned heard him murmur his name, and the faint voice replying something in the affirmative.

Mrs Simpson's appearance surprised Ned when he was admitted inside. She was sitting up in bed, pillows arranged comfortably behind her, and her hair done in its usual low style with a few curls hanging loose. But weariness was written all over her. It showed not so much in the lines of her face, which were still mostly, remarkably absent; it showed itself, rather, in the bewildered look in her eyes, in her absolute stillness, in the way that she turned her head only slightly in Ned's direction as he bowed.

"Master Ned," she pronounced. "I take it that there is no emergency with my will?"

"No," Ned admitted.

"Then you lied to gain admission? Well, well." A faint glimmer of amusement showed itself under her weariness. "Since you are here, we might as well have a talk."

Ned did as she said, sitting at the edge of the chair that was closest to her bedside. Mrs Simpson turned her head a little further in his direction, looking at him strangely, and he was beginning to wonder if he had sat in the wrong place when she said, thoughtfully, "In that very same spot before you this morning, Beatrice has sat, and my cousin Morgan after her."

"Please, ma'am," said Ned, grateful that she had steered them at once into the important subject. "You can't make her marry him."

"*Make* her?" Mrs Simpson's fair eyebrows rose a fraction. "I have no intention of 'making' Beatrice do anything. The choice is entirely hers – but if she wishes to save what's left of her reputation, marrying James Morgan is unfortunately the only thing she can do."

"Then you think it's unfortunate, too?" Ned seized on this, leaning so far forward in his chair in his eagerness that he was on the point of falling off outright. "Ma'am, I think there might be some things that you don't know about Mr Morgan..."

"Oh, I know everything there is to know about my cousin," she contradicted him, calmly.

"Then you must know that this has been his plan all along: to seduce Beatrice and marry her for money. He told me once..." Ned hesitated; it was one thing to relate Mr Morgan's words to Frank Allen, but quite another to repeat them in a lady's presence. He forced himself to go on. "He told me once that he would ruin her rather than let someone else marry her."

Mrs Simpson looked unsurprised. "Yes, that certainly sounds like something my cousin would say."

"Then you must know that you can't allow this!" Ned exclaimed, and then added hastily, "Ma'am. He has been planning this for years, and last night I am sure he took advantage of her: of her – her youth, her inexperience..."

"Oh, there is no doubt that he did. It has been rather disappointing for me, actually." Mrs Simpson shifted on her bedclothes. "I thought I had taught her better than that – taught her to be immune from the advances of men such as Morgan. But he dazzled her, she succumbed, and now what else is there to be done but get them married as soon as possible?"

"He cares nothing for her –"

"On the contrary," said Mrs Simpson, smiling as though he had just said something very amusing. "He cares a great deal for Beatrice. Just this morning, he sat in that very same seat and laid out all her innumerable charms for me. Chief among them being, though of course he wouldn't admit this, that when I die, Beatrice will be his ticket to an easy life. When he is married to her – of course, he didn't say this, either – he need never work another day in his life."

"Then you know that he is marrying her for money."

"What else would a man like Morgan think and plan for? Money is his greatest passion." Mrs Simpson watched him for a moment as he fidgeted in his seat. "I'm afraid, if you have come here merely to warn me about him, you have had a wasted journey."

"I have come," Ned said in a low voice, "because I thought you must care about Beatrice, and I *hoped* that you would care about her enough not to leave her to marry a fortune-hunter."

"It's certainly not what I planned, or hoped for her! Do you think I would have gone to all that expense and trouble to introduce her to society, merely to have her thrown away on *James Morgan?*" Mrs Simpson's tone had almost approached indignation, but now it became thoughtful once more. "But perhaps you don't know everything there is to know about him. Did you know, for instance, that they say he has made quite a bit of money in the war?"

"If he *has* made money," Ned said, thinking of Morgan at dinner last night, and the way the man's gaze had continually sought out Mrs Simpson, "then he has lost it again, somehow. Why else would he come back here?"

Mrs Simpson smiled for a second time. "How very astute you are, Master Ned. The very same thing crossed my mind, as soon as I heard that rumour about his supposed wealth. And then, of course, when we spoke earlier this morning, he spun some tales to me about the money he has made and how much he has distinguished himself, but I didn't believe a word. If that man has won independence, why would he come crawling back here like a cockroach?" She paused. "Then there is no reconciling you to his marriage with Beatrice, is there?"

"She can't marry him. You must find another way to fix this, to save her reputation..."

"Are you offering yourself?" Mrs Simpson interrupted, and Ned stared at her.

"What? No, I..."

"Then you *wouldn't* like to marry Beatrice?"

"I..." Ned felt his face heat under her gaze. He leaned back in his chair to put some distance between them. "I find her very – of course she is very beautiful and charming and if there ever was a chance..."

"*This* is your chance," said Mrs Simpson, matter-of-factly. "Take it now, or regret it for the rest of your life. Beatrice thinks she has no choice but to marry Morgan. But *you* are here: you have heard about the rumour and it still hasn't changed your feelings, has it?"

Ned shook his head slowly.

"Find Beatrice," Mrs Simpson instructed him. "Lay it all out before her as you just laid it out before me. Show her what Morgan is really after. Offer yourself as an alternative."

"But she doesn't... she doesn't care for me..."

"Perhaps not yet. But she will be grateful towards you for saving her – and other feelings can grow from gratitude. And anyway, whether she cares for you or not, she will be yours."

Ned's heart was beating so hard by now that he could feel a pulsing in his fingertips. There were protests that he knew he ought to make. There was the fact that he had come here with no other view than to save Beatrice from marrying Mr Morgan – certainly not with the view of advancing his own suit. There was his feeling that, even in the present circumstances, if he were to offer his hand to Beatrice, she would still laugh at him and disdain him. There was the matter of his still having an uncertain future, and nothing of substance to offer Beatrice. But over all these arguments, the voice of his own thwarted passion seemed to shout louder than the rest. This was the chance, that elusive *chance* that he had dreamt of for years! Wouldn't he be a fool not to take it now? Wasn't Mrs Simpson right, that he would regret it for the rest of his life?

"I am tired," Mrs Simpson's voice broke in on his reverie. "And I think, by looking at you, that you have already made your mind up. So I will ask you to leave me now."

"Of course." Ned scrambled to his feet in some confusion. "I'm sorry for – for lying about the will."

"'All's fair in love and war'," Mrs Simpson quoted, and Ned, unsure whether this meant that he was forgiven or not, unsure whether or not she might still be laughing at him, could think of no response to make. He got to his feet and bowed again.

"Good luck, Master Ned," were her parting words to him, and Ned, thanking her, did not know that it was the last time they would ever speak to one another.

He hurried down the corridor, pausing at the door that stood open to Beatrice's room, and ascertaining at a glance that it was still empty. He rushed on, down the stairs to the next floor, where he paused again at the door that led to the drawing room. The sound of music drifted out to greet him: Beatrice was playing piano, and when there came no break in the music at the sound of his knock, Ned knew that she must not have heard him. He was about to knock again when the music did stop, and in its place he heard voices.

"I've told you," Beatrice was saying to Mr Morgan, when Ned silently pushed open the door of the drawing room, just wide enough to see what was going on inside. "I've told you that you mustn't..."

"But how can any man resist, when he hears your siren song?" Morgan was standing over her at the piano, with one hand propped on the instrument and the other resting on Beatrice's upper back. He leaned in as though to kiss her – Ned's stomach lurched – and Beatrice leaned away.

"I must finish this piece," she said.

"Don't pretend to be taking your practice seriously now, when you never cared a jot for that instrument before. You funny, contrary creature. When we are married, I shall expect your full and undivided attention, you know."

Beatrice murmured something that Ned couldn't hear, but it seemed to please Mr Morgan, who said, "Yes, my darling. Whatever you like." He bent, and Beatrice dodged the attempt to kiss her once again, but this time, her head having been brought into a new angle, Ned could see that she was smiling.

Beatrice resumed her playing, in a fragmented, distracted way, all the more so once Mr Morgan seated himself beside her on the stool and began to press piano keys at random. Beatrice's attempts to ward him off only seemed to encourage him, as he pressed still more keys and stole an arm around her waist, which, in turn, caused *her* to laugh, and it was with the sound of those giggles still echoing in his ears that Ned Hyland finally absented himself.

Frank was still hanging around Mr Perry's office when Ned got back. "Well," he said, springing up from the desk. "You weren't as long as I thought you'd be. I've sent little Collins home and offered to finish off the copying for your uncle myself. Free of charge, for old-time's sake, you know. But – well – you're going to see him now?"

"Yes," said Ned, hoping his voice would not betray him as he moved for the stairs. "And after that, I'm going home."

It took him five minutes to say farewell – Mr Perry, being naturally unsuspicious, saw nothing amiss in his nephew's early return home. Another five minutes was sufficient to pack his bag, and then Ned descended the stairs, taking them two at a time, despising himself and his surroundings, and seeking to change one since he did not know how to change the other.

Frank was nowhere to be found in the office, but Ned met him outside on the street. "You're going to King's Cross?" Frank said, and when Ned confirmed this, offered to walk him there.

The rain from earlier had softened to a light drizzle, and the cool, gentle drops against his face gave some relief. But as they walked, Ned listened to Frank's silence and dreaded the moment when he would open a conversation. He knew that Frank had been wanting to talk to him about his workers' newspaper, and the state of affairs in Durham. Ned, who would have been ill-equipped for such a conversation at the best of times – his father being staunchly anti-union, and having imparted to Ned some of the same suspicions – under the present circumstances felt that it would have made impossible demands on him.

When Frank did speak up, though, it was to say, quietly, "You won't feel like this forever, you know."

Ned, watching the slap of the Thames against the landing stages below – the waters grey like the skies above – was unconvinced.

"I suppose you got turned down," Frank pursued, and though he sounded interested, there was none of his usual eagerness when talking of the affairs of others. His matter-of-fact manner seemed to suggest that Ned could say as little, or as much, as he liked; that he could say nothing at all and Frank would not think any the less of him.

"It's worse than that," Ned said hoarsely, thinking of Mrs Simpson telling him to find Beatrice – and what he had ended up *finding*, when he had come to the drawing room. He sensed Frank glance at him. "Because it's all been one big joke. A joke I keep falling for."

"Well," said Frank, after a pause. "What sort of people are they, to joke about things like that?"

"It's not Beatrice's fault," said Ned, surprised to find a

strand of loyalty still intact under the hurt and betrayal. "It's everyone around her."

"The old lady?"

Ned nodded. "And that man Morgan, and all those people who talk about nothing but money and appearances. They've made it so that those are the only things she cares about, too."

"Or maybe it's just the way she is," Frank said.

"No, she's more than that," Ned insisted. "And if she was around good people, people who brought out the best in her..."

"People like you?" But here Ned quickly shook his head.

"I'm past that now. I won't fool myself anymore about her. I won't think that way ever again."

"Good," said Frank, a little awkwardly. "I mean: these things have to end sometime. If you..." He stopped short, cursing, as the wheels of a passing carriage splashed through a puddle and sprayed him with dirty drops. "Well, that's just – anyway, if you're past thinking of her in that way, maybe you should also stop thinking you can help her somehow."

"But she has no one in the world who really cares about her. Not even Mrs Simpson – you should have seen how calmly she was talking today, knowing that Morgan's only marrying Beatrice for the inheritance and not caring..."

"Has she ever asked you for help?" Frank said. "Beatrice?"

"No, but –"

"Then maybe she needs it, but it's not up to you to give it." Frank hesitated, patting down his trousers absent-mindedly as they walked. "Or maybe – maybe she doesn't need it at all. Maybe she's happy with her life the way it is. You say there's no one who really cares for her – but maybe there's no one she really cares for, either, so it all evens out."

Ned was silent. That one word of Frank's – *happy* – had twisted something deep inside him. Was Beatrice happy, to be shackled into marriage with Mr Morgan? How could she be? And yet, when he had heard her laughing today, in that man's arms...

"Maybe..." he began, and then stopped, without any idea of what he had been going to say. He sensed Frank glance at him. Ned sighed. "What's the use? I can't make sense of any of it now."

"Wait till you get home," Frank agreed. "Think it over. Think about whether she's worth wasting any more time over – especially now that she's getting married. Think about other things you might spend your time doing."

And, to Frank Allen's credit, that was the only hint he dropped about the newspaper for the duration of their walk to the station. The rest of it passed in silence. When they parted ways on the platform, Frank handed Ned his address with the suggestion to write whenever he felt like it. But no more mention was made of the matter, and Ned was left feeling not quite as miserable as before. For the first time, he could see a future without Beatrice. Dull and featureless it might be, and very unlike any of the stories in his books, but he could picture it now where he hadn't been able to before. That had to mean something.

5

LAST WILL AND TESTAMENT

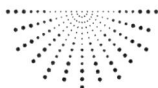

1 *856*

The next time that Ned Hyland visited London, which was the following summer, it was not for the purpose of seeing Beatrice or Mrs Simpson or any of the people connected with the house in Highgate – even his uncle. Concerning that part of Ned's world, and the various lives that orbited around Mrs Simpson's cold, bright star, he felt, at most, a distant curiosity. He had endeavoured for a long time to stop caring about those people, and was really starting to believe that he had succeeded.

His visit to London that summer was, instead, the conclusion of a two-month-long tour which he and Frank Allen had undertaken. The tour had brought them through England, Scotland, Wales and even parts of Ireland. Their time in Ireland they had found the most sobering; the countryside, left in the wake of a devastating famine, had seemed half-deserted. But in every place that they had visited on their tour, from country hamlets to manufacturing towns to port cities, Ned and Frank had interviewed workers and written up reports. Their observations were to form part of a book by Mr Charles Low, the editor of the newspaper where Frank worked.

Some of the expenses of the long tour had been paid for them by Mr Low, while others had not. Ned's mother had given him a little something towards the tour – his father, who thoroughly disapproved of the whole venture, had not – and though the newspaper paid him to write the occasional article, it was nothing like a regular salary. Accordingly, Ned found himself returning to London with light pockets, and it was out of necessity more than anything else that he came to stay with his uncle Perry. There was no way he could afford a hotel, and no one he could stay with: Frank, who had had to give up his rented room when they went on the tour, was staying with the Lows until he could find somewhere else, and Ned couldn't very well impose on them too.

He would have avoided such an arrangement, had he had the means to do so. It was not that he was afraid of what might happen if he stayed with Uncle Perry. Should any hint of that other world – the Highgate world – drift to his ears, Ned would simply adopt his tried and tested policy of the last eight months, and feign deafness and blindness. He knew that he would not allow himself to become entangled with Beatrice and Mrs Simpson again. What he dreaded, instead, was the careless reference, the kind of aside that one could not possibly plan for. Such an aside might issue from Mr Perry, or Miss Pleasant, or the young clerk, Collins, or from some other source that Ned had not even considered.

In Durham and on his tour, Ned had been sheltered from casual gossip about Mr and Mrs Morgan. Frank had kept a tactful silence, only telling him that Beatrice and Mr Morgan had been married last January, that Mrs Simpson was still alive and that everyone was still dancing to her tune. But now that Ned was in London again, he felt that he had stepped back out onto exposed terrain. An enemy might strike him now, from any direction, and set him back weeks in his progress. Hearing that Beatrice was with child, for example, or even that she was blissfully happy (though he did not wish her to be *unhappy*, either, Ned often tried to tell himself) would, after the exertions of the last few months, wreak havoc with his nerves.

He entered Mr Perry's house, therefore, in a state of trepidation, which took a day or so to diminish. Bit by bit, though, he saw that he had nothing to fear from his uncle, who, apart from asking Ned a few questions about Mr Low's book, and yawning over the answers, broached no other topics more dangerous than the heat of the city in August, or the impossibility of working without a clerk.

Fred Collins was on holiday in Plymouth, a fact which Mr Perry faintly resented, himself holding it as a matter of pride that he had never been seduced away from his desk to the temptations of "the seaside".

Ned only planned to be in London for a week at most, during which time he and Frank would carry out some final interviews to add to Mr Low's book. Mr Perry, in general, showed little interest in Ned's comings and goings, but one evening, as his nephew was passing through his office on his way to meet Frank, he surprised him with a remark on his attire.

"You're not going out in that?"

Ned turned back, raising his arms from his sides and looking down at the peacoat that he had put on. "What, you mean this?"

"It looks worn out," said Mr Perry doubtfully.

"It *is* worn out," Ned admitted. "I wore it all through the tour."

"You'd better borrow something of mine." His uncle began to raise himself from his desk.

"Really, I wouldn't worry about it," Ned said, putting up his hands. "I'm just meeting Frank at the Lows'."

"Didn't you say Mr Low has a daughter?"

"Well – yes, he does, but..." Ned couldn't help smiling, at

the notion of his dressing to impress the stern and serious Miss Low.

"It's settled, then. You'll wear something of mine for this evening." His uncle shuffled towards the stairs. Over his shoulder, he called, "And tomorrow, first thing, you'll buy a new coat."

"I haven't got the money," Ned called back, and his uncle stopped in his tracks, turning at the foot of the stairs.

"Haven't got the money?" he repeated, looking scandalised. "What do you mean?" He took a few steps closer to Ned, tilting his head as though struck by a new, disturbing thought. "You don't... gamble, do you?"

"No, uncle," Ned sighed.

"Is it drinking, then? I've heard of many young men..."

"No, I spent my money on travelling. That's all."

"Travelling?" Mr Perry, judging by his expression, seemed to consider this the worst explanation of all. "But didn't you plan what you ought to spend ahead of time?"

"I tried to, but things just... got away from me."

Mr Perry examined him for a moment more. "People oughtn't to travel at all if they know they can't afford it."

"I realise that *now*," Ned said, "But it seemed so important at the time, what we were doing."

"Money is important, too," his uncle pointed out. "And having enough of it to turn yourself out well – or afford a decent coat, at least."

Ned nodded, as there was no part of this speech with which he could argue: it was all plain, good sense. "I'll be more careful in the future."

"Hmph." His uncle, though evidently not satisfied with the answer, left it until the following morning to bring up the matter again – whereupon he informed Ned that he would give him a pound to buy a new coat, if Ned, in return, did a few errands for him that would ordinarily have fallen on the absent Collins's shoulders.

"Carrying letters here and there across town," was how his uncle described these errands. "Writing out invoices and receipts." Nothing was mentioned about the house in Highgate. And it was not until the following day that Ned found himself confronting the very situation that he had been hoping to avoid. Mrs Simpson had requested to add a codicil to her will, and Mr Perry wanted to send her a confirmation that it had indeed been added. Ned did not know the details of the said codicil, and did not need to know them; he only knew that, since the confirmation was apparently too sensitive to be delivered by post, his uncle preferred to have Ned deliver it by hand – which meant that he was to revisit the scene of his own humiliation and heartbreak, not as a conquering hero returned from abroad, but as an errand boy.

It was unlikely that he would meet Beatrice in Highgate. Ned recalled Frank telling him that after her marriage, she and James Morgan had moved to accommodations in Soho. Still, the very act of his going to Mrs Simpson's house opened him to the possibility of seeing Beatrice again. Yet he had made no objections when his uncle had asked him to carry the all-important letter there. Was this because he was too honourable to go back on his word, even though this particular errand was one that he knew he should not carry out? Or was it because there was a small part of him, whose existence he had denied over the last eight months, still alive with foolish hope and useless ardour? Ned tried to examine his own motivations on the way to Highgate, but the carriage ride was not nearly long enough to allow for the many turnings of his mind.

Though he was left waiting for some time after ringing the bell, he did not attempt to climb the gate, as he had done last winter. He was on official business now, not on some quest of the heart. When the maid appeared – a new face – Ned announced himself but made no other attempt at conversation, following her up the drive and feeling, as he had often done before, that a thousand pairs of eyes were watching him, from the dark depths of the house's many windows.

"You'd better watch your step here," advised the young

maid as they came into the dimly-lit hall. "The mistress likes to save on candles..."

"Yes," said Ned. "I know."

Mrs Simpson was not fit to receive visitors, according to the maid. Rather than being brought upstairs to the drawing room, Ned was instead shown into the formal parlour, and told to wait there in case Mrs Simpson should want to send a reply to Mr Perry's letter of acknowledgement. He did so most unwillingly. Not only was he reluctant to prolong his time at Highgate – and thereby increase the danger of seeing the woman who now went by Mrs Morgan – but the parlour was a dusty, airless room. He had only been in it once before, on the night of the coming-out, and he had the feeling that it had not been opened or cleaned since then.

Resting himself tentatively on one of the armchairs, Ned sprang up again at the feeling of damp seeping into the fabric of his trousers, and chose to stand instead, leaning one arm against the mantlepiece and gazing down at the pile of old ashes in the grate. The romantic part of him could not resist connecting those ashes with his own extinguished hopes – both had burned their last that same night, the night of Beatrice's coming-out. The more reasonable, Mr Perry-ish part of him reflected that, if Beatrice did indeed inherit this house, as everyone expected her to, she would have her work cut out for her in attending to all this damp and neglect. Then again, Ned reminded himself, she had a husband who had made himself useful in the past when it came to Highgate's repairs, and could likely rise to the occasion again if so required.

Just as that last, painful thought of Mr Morgan's capabilities was passing through his mind, Ned turned at the sound of the parlour door, and was somewhat surprised to see Miss Simpson stepping in.

He had only glimpsed her at the coming-out last winter, and his main impression of her was still fixed at six years before. In the essentials, she was unchanged: her hair a little greyer, perhaps, her form thinner and her face more strained than it had been back then. But where her manner before had been all bustling activity, now her movements were slow and discreet. She held her skirts as she moved, as though worried that their rustle might disturb the delicate silence of the house. Her voice was hushed as she told Ned that Mrs Simpson saw no need to send a reply to his uncle, but would be glad to speak to *him* if he wished to step upstairs for a moment.

Ned hesitated. He did not like to refuse the summons of a sick woman – but all too fresh in his mind was the result of his last conversation with Mrs Simpson: his hopeful dash down to the drawing room, only to be greeted by the sight of Beatrice in Mr Morgan's arms, and to suffer the sound of her laughter. "You must thank her on my behalf, for her kindness," he said to Miss Simpson. "But I intended to leave a few minutes ago, and really should be on my way already."

Miss Simpson's expression clouded for a moment, in obvious confusion at anyone refusing to see Mrs Simpson when expressly asked. But she soon recovered herself, and bowed her head in gracious response.

"I certainly will, Mr Hyland. But – if I may ask, before you go, so that I might carry a report back to my sister-in-law – I hope you are well?"

Ned had to restrain a smile at the forced civility. "You may tell Mrs Simpson that I am very well," he said. Then, unable to resist, "And you may tell her that I am grateful for her wise words to me last winter. Although I was unable to follow her advice in the end, I trust that it was given in the full spirit of generosity that is so much her character."

Miss Simpson looked as though she did not quite understand this speech, and was therefore unsure how she would be able to relate back all its details to her mistress. After a moment's pause, she replied, "Yes, Arabella *is* so very generous: how right you are, young man."

Ned made a motion as if to go, but Miss Simpson's voice called him back.

"Don't you want to hear about Miss Smith?" As Ned turned around, she corrected herself, "Mrs Morgan, I should say. You know that she is married?"

Ned nodded. His own voice seemed to come from somewhere distant as he said, "I hope she is well."

"Oh, she is – or as well as can be expected after making such an unfortunate match. We had all hoped for better for her, of course. And for a while at first we thought that James Morgan had made some money abroad – *that* would have been something, at least – but then it turned out that he lost it all at the card-tables. So you see, Beatrice will have to scrimp and save, as I keep telling her, but it is so difficult for those who have no experience of managing their own expenses to begin from scratch! I hear that even her dowry has been spent already, though whether by him or her I don't know; and they have had to move more than once since they got married, on account of not being able to afford the rent, you see..." Miss Simpson paused to draw breath. She had two spots of colour in her cheeks and was evidently enjoying herself – no doubt she did not often get the chance these days to talk about Beatrice to an interested but ignorant party such as Ned. "Well, it is a pity, at any rate. When she might have had anyone –"

"I heard," Ned interrupted, "that she didn't have much choice in the matter."

Miss Simpson, far from looking shame-faced, nodded earnestly. "Well, that is true – once she had behaved as she behaved at her coming-out, there was not much choice but to have her marry Mr Morgan, but my sister-in-law and I feel it all might have been avoided. We think we might have guided her better, to avoid such pitfalls..."

"Or perhaps if people did not like to gossip so much," Ned said pointedly. "Miss Smith – I mean Mrs Morgan would not have had to marry so soon as she did."

But Miss Simpson was apparently oblivious to his hints. "Oh yes, it is dreadful how quickly a rumour spreads, particularly when it is about a beautiful young lady like Mrs Morgan – and one under Mrs Simpson's care, too, which no doubt added to people's interest in the affair! And there is really nothing worse than a hasty marriage. I am sure she will regret it for the rest of her life."

There was something about the way she said that last sentence, almost with an air of relish, which determined Ned not to listen to any more. "Please remember me to her," he told Miss Simpson, briefly, "the next time you see her. And now I really must be going."

Ned wondered whether it was his fate, every time he passed within the walls of this house, to come away dismayed or disgusted with what he had found. He loathed Morgan more than anything else – but what right had Miss Simpson to criticise Beatrice's choice, after she had made it almost impossible for her to do anything else? She had been no friend to her, Ned thought, furiously, and then, struck by a sudden thought, he came to a halt in the middle of the drive.

Was it surprising that Miss Simpson had not been a good friend to Beatrice, when Beatrice had obviously had nothing but contempt for her? Perhaps she had learned that attitude from Mrs Simpson, but that did not make it any more excusable. And what was it Frank had said to him that time, walking him to the station the day after Beatrice's coming-out? *You say there's no one who really cares for her – but maybe there's no one she really cares for, either.*

Ned tried to remember whether he had ever seen evidence of Beatrice caring for anyone. She had always seemed devoted to Mrs Simpson, but maybe that was for the same reason that all the others *seemed* devoted to that lady: united by the hope of what they might get in the future. She had made her contempt for Miss Simpson very clear. As for Ned himself, Beatrice had kissed him once to say sorry for making him upset – but then she had run away laughing. How deeply could such feelings have really gone?

And then there was Mr Morgan. How did she feel about *him*? Ned began to walk again as he contemplated the question. A haze of anger and embarrassment still hung over his memory of seeing the two in the drawing room, the day he had learned of Beatrice's fate. Now he tried to see past that haze, to piece apart the scene for what it had really showed him. Had Beatrice really been happy – or had she been making the best of things? Had she loved Mr Morgan then – did she love him now? Miss Simpson had said that they had had to move lodgings more than once. And now that Mrs Simpson's health was failing, the question of her will must have come up more than once.

Might such trials have unveiled Mr Morgan's true character to Beatrice? *Maybe she knows already what he's like, what he's after*, said a Frank-like voice in Ned's head, *and doesn't care.*

The gate creaked behind Ned, and he stepped back out onto the road. It was a fine evening; he took in a great, gulping breath of air, held it for a moment and then released it. Already thoughts of Beatrice and Mr Morgan and the Simpsons seemed to be retreating to the edges of his mind, scattered by the bright summer sun. He turned his back on the house in Highgate, feeling some pride, and not a little relief, in the fact that he had gotten away without seeing her, or either of them. Perhaps he would walk back to Mr Perry's. Tomorrow he had a busy day of interviews. The day after, he and Frank would write them up and submit them to Mr Low's office. And the day after that – Ned would be going home to Durham.

When he was a little way down the road, a carriage passed close by him. Ned paid it no heed, apart from shrinking back a little from its proximity. It was a minute or two afterwards that he heard the sounds of a commotion, looked back to see that the carriage was a cab, and that it had parked right outside the gates of Mrs Simpson's house. A dark-haired young woman had just stepped out, but as Ned watched, the driver climbed down from his box and restrained her by the arm. The two struggled for a moment, and Ned broke into a stride, then a run.

"Please let go of me," he heard the woman's calm voice, once he got close enough to hear and make out what they were saying. "I've told you twice and I won't tell you again. Fancy making such a fuss over a few shillings! You must just let me go inside to fetch the rest of the fare and then I'll bring it right out to you..."

"I've heard that before," growled the driver. "I wasn't born yesterday, you know!"

"You're really being most unreasonable – surely my word should be enough?"

"Your word isn't worth –" began the driver, but he did not get to finish the insult, because Ned, panting, had drawn up beside them.

"Excuse me, sir, how much is the lady short?"

They both turned to stare at him. "Five shillings," said the driver, and Ned felt in his pocket. He still had some change from the money Mr Perry had given him for his new coat. He counted out the coins and handed the sum over.

The driver muttered his thanks and got back on his box without another glance at Beatrice. For the woman *was* Beatrice Morgan: more sheepish than Ned had ever seen her looking before, her smooth white face now hewn with new cares, but all the more beautiful for it. Her dark hair was swept above her head in a new style, and her eyes still as bright – though as soon as Ned met their astonished gaze, they dropped from his view, screened by dark lashes until he could make out nothing of their expression anymore.

"Thank you, Mr Hyland," said Beatrice, without looking at him. "You were just coming to visit Mrs Simpson?"

"I was just going," Ned corrected her, and turned away as though to confirm his words. But a gloved hand reached out to grab his arm to stop him, and to Ned's unbelieving ears came words that he never thought he would hear.

"Please – oh, please," said Beatrice, "don't go just yet."

❧

Beatrice had been about to pay a visit to her old home, but she was more than happy to defer that visit for a little while in order to talk to Ned, as she now told him frankly. "Especially now I know that *she's* still there," Beatrice said – the *she* in this case referring to Miss Simpson. "I thought she would have gone back to Dover by now, to wait it out there instead. Who knows when it might be, after all? Another six months, maybe even a year. She's held out longer than anyone thought."

Ned was silent. They had left the road, and were walking along a path chosen by Beatrice. It was cool and woody, and led eventually, or so Beatrice had said, into Hampstead Heath. Ned had never been to this part of Highgate before, and had only been dimly aware of it.

"It's something, to breathe fresh, green air, isn't it?" Beatrice said, turning her face up to the canopy of leaves overhead. "I don't get a lot of it these days."

Looking sidelong at her, Ned thought there must be many other things that Beatrice was missing these days, too – rest and ease being among them. The signs of nervous strain were written all over her: in her new pallor, in the purple shadows under her eyes, and in the way those eyes frequently darted away from his, where they had once met Ned's with careless confidence. Noting all of this, he suddenly felt very sorry for her, and was then surprised by how the feeling seemed to blot out all else, as though all of his old longing and desire had been set down for the moment.

"You must think I'm awful," said Beatrice, breaking the silence. "Talking of Mrs Simpson in this way – as if she's a ticking clock. But it's the way James talks of her, you see, and I think he's got me into the habit of it, too." She turned to look at Ned. "Sometimes we feel like we've been waiting for ever so long. And – you see – it's so hard to plan anything, to make changes, until we know..."

"Until you know what you're getting?" Ned prompted, and Beatrice nodded.

"James thinks it will be the house. I'm not so sure – but he says there's no question about it. He says, why else would Mrs Simpson have taken me in all those years ago, and gone to such trouble to bring me up as a lady, if she didn't intend on providing for me in the end? But what *I* say is, she might just as well provide for me with a sum of money as with the house. And I think it's more likely to be money, for me – I think the house will go to someone in her family."

"You should know," Ned said, after a moment's deliberation, "that Mrs Simpson has added a codicil to her will. I came to Highgate today on behalf of my uncle to deliver his confirmation letter." Hearing Beatrice eagerly draw breath, as though on the point of asking a question, he pressed on quickly, "I don't know the details. I only know that she requested for it to be added recently."

"A codicil," repeated Beatrice, and subsided into silence for a few minutes. The trees on the path around them had begun to retreat, and spaces of green park were now visible between the branches; Ned even glimpsed, in the distance, the gleam of sunlight on what looked like a pond. "I wonder," said Beatrice, and he glanced back at her. She was frowning deeply. "I wonder if it can be – but I'll have to explain to you first. You see, I asked to borrow money from Mrs Simpson a little while ago. Not very much – just a hundred pounds."

Ned raised his eyebrows at Beatrice's idea of "not very much".

"Just to get James out of a bit of trouble," Beatrice pursued. "There's this fellow he plays cards with, you see, who always cheats, but no one has the nerve to say it to this man's face, because he is very strong and intimidating – and anyway, since he won the game, James owes him money, even though if they had been playing fair and square, it would have been the other way around..."

"And has Mrs Simpson lent you the hundred pounds yet?"

"Not yet. That was what I was coming to see her today about. But I was hoping I wouldn't have to do it in front of Eliza Simpson – in fact, I think it's Eliza who probably told her not to lend it to me straight away, to make me wait instead. The last time..."

"You've borrowed money from her before?"

"Yes, a few months back. Only fifty pounds then, and she gave it straight away. I was quick about paying her back, too. But this time, she has made me wait a little longer. I hope she'll give it to me today – but I'd prefer to wait a little while before I go to ask her. I don't like doing these things."

"No one does," Ned said quietly.

They had come out into an open space, and Beatrice took a few steps more before halting at a nearby bench, and gesturing to it. "Let's sit for a minute, will we? What a nice view this is."

Ned followed her gaze. The path that they had been following had wound along a gentle slope, and they were at some height now. Green hills fell away before them, dotted here and there with walking figures. The city sprawled somewhere behind those hills, but the only hint of its presence was the smoke on the horizon; from this distance, the smoke looked blue and almost pretty.

Beatrice sat, arranging her skirts carefully, and Ned, with a glance at her attire, took a seat at the other end of the bench. It struck him that, even in dire financial straits, Mrs Morgan was still well-turned out: her shoes were polished and gleaming as though brand new, her blue muslin dress was smooth and uncreased, and though its high collar and long sleeves must have been uncomfortable in the heat, she held herself as though she was perfectly at ease. Remembering Mr Perry's lecture from a few days before on his ragged coat, Ned couldn't help smiling, thinking that his uncle would whole-heartedly approve of Beatrice's sense of priorities in this case.

"I'm not keeping you from anything, am I?" said Beatrice, a new note of anxiety in her tone that was entirely foreign to Ned's ears. He had turned his head away to hide his smile, but she seemed to have attributed the movement to some other source of distraction.

"No, you're not," Ned assured her, turning back so that they were face to face again. Beatrice smiled in relief, hastily dropping her gaze from his as he continued to look at her, and for a minute or two they sat in silence, listening to the buzzing of insects in the grass and the call of birds in the little wood that they had just left behind.

The air around them was laden with sweetness and heavy with warmth.

"I wonder," Beatrice said at length, "if Mrs Simpson has added that codicil to her will because of the money I asked to borrow." As Ned looked at her questioningly, she continued, "Even though I said I'd pay it back – maybe she doesn't believe I will. Well, you know how she counts every penny! Think of how she's always tried to save on candles – *candles*, which are as cheap as dirt. Suppose she's added that codicil to her will to deduct the amount I asked, a hundred pounds, from whatever sum she's decided to give me!"

Ned crossed one leg over the other as he considered this. "Even if that's the case," he said, shading his eyes with his hand as he looked at Beatrice, which was necessary, since the sun had just emerged from a cloud behind her and was bathing her in light, "you'll still get the rest of the money."

"But when?" Beatrice persisted. "And *how much*? And – oh..." She broke off, shaking her head. "There I go again, talking about money when I might be talking about much nicer things, on a day like this, with *you*! Oh, I wish there was no such thing as money in the world! It seems to turn us all into the lowest creatures that crawl the earth, when we don't have enough of it!"

"Not you," Ned said quietly. He sensed her looking at him, but this time it was he who could not meet her gaze.

"You're wrong," said Beatrice, after a moment. "I'm the lowest of all of them. I sometimes think... I sometimes wish Mrs Simpson had left me where she had found me. Then at least I would have had the kind of life I was supposed to have, even if it was just begging on the streets. Trouble is, I don't remember enough about that life, the life I had before she took me in, I mean: it doesn't seem real to me anymore."

Ned reached across the bench and took her hand. The move was instinctive. He had done so once before, years ago, prompted by the same instinct that moved him now: the idea that somehow, by taking her hand, he might protect her from her own thoughts, or from the dark forces that swirled around her. Back then, she had shrunk from his touch and run from him: this time, he sensed her hesitate, and then respond in kind, her gloved fingers curving around the back of his hand.

It was a moment or two before reality crashed in on upon him. Then Ned saw all at once what he was doing. He dropped Beatrice's hand as though it had burned him. "I'm sorry. I wasn't thinking –"

"You have nothing to be sorry for," he heard Beatrice say, but Ned could not look at her now: he averted his gaze from the sun and from her, keeping both in his peripheral vision as he got to his feet.

"I'd better be going now," he said, for a second time, turning from her but waiting, just a fraction of a second.

If she asked him to stay again, he knew that he would. What kind of person did that make him?

But Beatrice did not ask him to stay, and Ned left her on the bench, hurrying back along the path they had just taken, tripping over roots and stones. It was as though he thought, if he moved fast enough, and far enough away, the moment in the park could be denied – packed away among many things that might have been rather than things that were.

~

It would never have occurred to Beatrice that there could be anything wrong in Ned Hyland taking her hand – or, at least, it did not occur to her to see anything else in the gesture until he had gotten up and run away, leaving her alone in the park. Then, after wallowing for a few minutes in her own disappointment and loneliness – two emotions that had become very familiar to her over the last eight months – she thought for a time about Ned, about how sweet and honest he had always been, and how little a man like him would expect or desire to be dragged into a flirtation with a married woman.

What embarrassed Beatrice was that her behaviour, in accepting what had only seemed to her at the time a gesture of friendship, might have made Ned think that she was open to the possibility of such a flirtation. She knew that people still talked about her, even if her speedy marriage to James had dampened most of those rumours. James himself had accused her a few times of "making eyes" at other men – men on the street, men in shops and even on occasion a couple of friends from his club that he had brought home. Beatrice had not been aware, at any of these times, of showing any more attention to these men than what was strictly civil on her part.

But James's comments had made her take greater care in how she spoke and looked at men, and when Ned Hyland had come to her rescue so unexpectedly earlier, she had been struck with a strange shyness. This stemmed partly from her newfound fear of "making eyes", and partly from the impression that Ned had grown a couple of inches taller since last winter, or somehow aged a few years in the space of months, or both. When those grey eyes looked at Beatrice now, they seemed to be looking a little past her – which was simultaneously frustrating and fascinating.

Her shyness had lasted throughout most of their walk, but once they were sitting on the bench, and she heard his quiet, steady voice assuring her that she was not the low creature she had declared herself to be – Beatrice felt as though they were both children again. Nothing had really changed since then, it seemed; Ned still thought the world of her, thanks to no particular effort on Beatrice's part. And when he took her hand, it seemed the natural progression of that realisation. There no fear that such an action could progress any further, even though she had responded in kind. She was sure that Ned would not try to kiss her, or do anything else alarming. So why had he run away from her, as though faced with some great danger?

Beatrice wondered, as she made her way home, whether she ought to tell James about what had happened. She thought about how *she* would feel if some woman had taken James's hand – and, in the lash of fury that went through her, had her answer then and there. But what if James did something to Ned? How would she make him see how innocent it had felt at the time, or how Ned had seemed so worried and sorry afterwards?

Having borrowed the fare from Miss Simpson – a necessity that seemed crueller than any other Beatrice had been forced on thus far – she was not accosted this time by the cab driver, but set down very civilly on the pavement in front of the terraced house in Farringdon. Beatrice and James had the two upper floors of the house, and another family occupied the lower two. It was not as nice as their lodgings in Soho, which they had had entirely to themselves, but not as squalid as the boarding house in Hackney where they had spent a month, in the time between being forced out of Soho and finding this place.

There was a girl who was supposed to come and clean during the afternoons, but Beatrice saw, as soon as she had turned the key in the door and looked down their narrow, cluttered hallway, that the girl had decided to take the day off. There was nothing Beatrice could say or do when such things happened; she had lost her last two servants after chiding them for doing the very same thing, and knew that this girl would be ready to walk out at the first uncivil word. It was not as if, after all, she and James were paying her anything close to the normal rates for servants.

Beatrice untied the strings of her bonnet and hung it on a hook beside the door. Then, stepping carefully through the hall, kicking James's stray pairs of boots aside as she went, she called out, "Darling?"

"Darling!" came the response, and James Morgan issued forth from a door to their left, which led to his bedroom. He was in his shirtsleeves, and had some ink spots on his fingers, as though he had been writing a letter when she interrupted him. "How was the old lady?"

"Very weak. I only stayed five minutes – Eliza Simpson was hanging around."

"Odious old spinster," James said comfortably, and kissed Beatrice. She wound her arms around his neck, but he pulled back almost right away and asked, "Did you get the hundred pounds?"

"Not quite yet," Beatrice said sheepishly, and watched as James sighed, rubbing his neck. "Mrs Simpson said she will send it soon."

"Send it? Why couldn't she just give it to you? You were

right there – that was the idea of going to see her, wasn't it?"

"Not just that, dear. Of course it is my duty to go and see her when she is sick, to see if there is anything I can do for her, after all that she has done for me…"

"All that she has done for you?" James repeated in disbelief, and shook his head. "The best thing she could do for you now is –" But, seeing the expression on Beatrice's face, he stopped short and turned back for the bedroom. "I thought something like this would happen," he said over his shoulder. "Which is why I'm in the middle of writing to one of my fellow officers from abroad. He was a good sort of fellow – reliable. Won't begrudge me a small sum like a hundred pounds, though I daresay he can't spare it nearly as well as my old cousin can." With another sigh, "I only hope he hasn't changed address since he came back to England."

Beatrice, who had bent down to start rearranging the boots in the hall into neat pairs, said nothing. A moment later, James reappeared in the doorway and said, "By the way, the girl's handed in her notice."

"What girl?" Beatrice's head snapped up.

"I don't know her name. The girl who used to come here to clean."

"Lily," Beatrice said, rising to her feet again.

"Yes, that was it, I suppose."

"But why would she give her notice? I've never said a harsh word to her – never laid down the law..."

"She said she can 'make much more working for real gentlefolk'," James told her, mimicking the girl's accents. "I suppose we don't count." With another shrug, he disappeared into his room again. Beatrice, left standing in the hall, put a hand to her forehead, where she could feel the beginnings of a headache starting up.

"I'd better start cooking dinner," she called through the gap in the door, but James called back,

"Oh, never mind about me, darling! I'll be eating out."

"At your club?" Beatrice asked.

"Yes, we have a good game planned for tonight."

"Please..." Beatrice started, and then stopped. She said a moment later, a little lamely, "Please be careful."

There was a creak as James rose from his chair, crossed the room and came to face her. "I'm always careful, Beatrice," he said, looking down at her with an expression that was half-exasperated, half-affectionate, and – it struck Beatrice, with a pang – completely lacking in passion. How could he look at her so differently now from how he had looked at her that night at her coming-out, or the day after, when he had proposed, or the day of their wedding? How could so much have changed between them in so little time?

"But, you know," James went on, patting her cheek in an absent-minded kind of gesture, "I can't help it when other men cheat at cards. I can only try my best to be an honourable player, as I always do."

"Yes," said Beatrice, flatly, and he let go of her, retreating into his room. When, an hour later, she heard the sound of the slamming door, it was the only announcement of his going that she had had. He had not come into the kitchen to say goodnight to her.

∼

After parting from Beatrice in Hampstead Heath, it took Ned the whole walk back to town to sort out the mess in his head. Then he saw his own foolishness, how, once again, he had fallen into a trap of his own making. He should never have agreed to carry his uncle's letter to Highgate in the first place – and, having got there, he should never have agreed to walk with Beatrice. Paying her cab fare should have been more than sufficient. She was a married woman, and though she might need help now more than ever before, he was not the one who could give it to her. Frank had been right, back then, in what he had said. Ned had to stop thinking that he could protect Beatrice, or even love her in his own, quiet way; she had moved too far away even for him to do the latter.

For his last few days in London, Ned sank once more into the work that had occupied him so completely for the past few months. Between meeting Frank and the Lows, he carried out whatever errands were left for him to do, and on the day of his departure, was in time to see Mr Perry's clerk Collins return to his desk. Thus it was with a faint satisfaction and sense of completion that Ned departed London. He did not plan to be back for some months at least, and did not imagine that there would be much work for him at the newspaper in the intervening time. If his father could get a place for him at the mine again, Ned would take all the hours that he could get, to fill up his pockets and regain some measure of independence. Beatrice had said it best: it would have been better if there were no such thing as money in the world, but so long as there *was*, it would not really be possible for Ned to choose what he wanted to do.

At home, with this new awareness, he meekly submitted to lectures first from his mother and then from his father, both of whom he had disappointed in different ways. To Mrs Hyland, the law was the perfect alternative to dirty mine work, and she could not understand why Ned should turn his nose up at it; to Mr Hyland, it was all too clear that his son had been gallivanting and shilly-shallying all over the kingdom, and only chosen to come back to his responsibilities once his pockets were empty. A job at the mine he would have: Mr Hyland would arrange it, but not without giving his eldest son an earful first. Ned had just resigned himself to months of "I told you so"s when a letter arrived for him from London, addressed in Beatrice's hand.

It was not even a fortnight since he had left. Ned tore open the envelope and read that Mrs Simpson had passed away. He spent a long time composing his own reply, thanking Beatrice for telling him, expressing his condolences for her loss and his regrets that his work schedule would not allow him to attend the funeral. It was the question of how to sign off the letter that gave him the most difficulty; he spun his pen around in his hand for some immeasurable time, and at length scribbled, "Your friend, always, Ned."

A day later, another letter arrived for Ned, this time from Mr Perry. Unaware that Ned had already received an account from Beatrice, his uncle informed that Mrs Simpson had died in her sleep on the weekend, and that the funeral was to be held the following day and that Ned should attend if he could – but, as it was such short notice, he could be forgiven for missing it, as long as he attended the will-reading next Monday. Mrs Simpson had expressly requested that he be there.

The letter threw the Hyland household into disarray. "That old woman *can't* have left him anything," Mrs Hyland insisted, over and over again, though the light of hope in her eyes belied her words. "Really, I don't see how it's possible, with her own family and two sets of in-laws to remember, and that girl you told me about, the one that she adopted..."

As for Mr Hyland, while Ned's account of the house in Highgate had left him with no good opinion of its matriarch, he surprised his son with his grim insistence that he must go next Monday. "Don't stay the night: go down and come back in the one day – that way you won't lose too much time at work. But you'd better go all the same. She's asked for you to be there, and to ignore her would be disrespecting the dead."

It was only Ned who had any kind of grasp on the reality of the situation. He knew that Mrs Simpson's request was most likely to be a posthumous joke at his expense, and that he would be fully justified in ignoring it. He knew that to go back to London, for no other reason this time than to carry out Mrs Simpson's wishes, would be to plunge headfirst into the danger that he had escaped almost two weeks before. Who knew how he might betray himself this time, if he got carried away by his emotions? Perhaps he would not stop at taking Beatrice's hand. And what if Beatrice had told Morgan about Ned taking her hand? Was the man who had threatened an eleven-year-old boy likely to show any more restraint now that Ned was grown up?

At the edges of Ned's mind lurked a possibility that was crueller still: that Beatrice *had* told her husband about the moment between them at the park, and that they had both laughed over it, and that in showing up to the will-reading, Ned would be subjecting himself to their mutual disdain and amusement.

"I don't know what you're so nervous about," Mrs Hyland remarked, the night before Ned's departure. Seeing the light under his door, she had come in to find her son still fully awake, even though the church bell had struck midnight a half hour ago. "You barely said a word at dinner. Surely you don't think it can be bad news? What kind of person would summon someone to their will-reading only to tell them that they've got nothing?"

"It's not getting nothing I'm afraid of," Ned murmured. He was sitting at his desk. For the past hour, he had been sketching out an idea for an article for Mr Low's newspaper on the recent history of mine strikes in Northumberland and Durham. But now, looking down at his own cramped writing on the page, he felt that it was useless and cast the thing aside in disgust.

"What *are* you afraid of, then?" Mrs Hyland pursued. At her son's silence, she sighed. "Whatever it is, at least you know you'll never have to see these strange people again after tomorrow."

"I'd prefer never to have to see them again at all," said Ned.

"Well, that may be, but... your father's right. You've been asked, so you must go." His mother hesitated for a moment more on the threshold. "Try to get some sleep."

Despite her urging, Ned did not settle down to bed till hours later, when the sky was beginning to get light. It seemed that he had only had his eyes closed for five minutes when a knock sounded on his door, and his mother's voice summoned him to breakfast. From his pillows, Ned looked up at his damp-spotted ceiling, and wondered what changes might have wrought themselves upon him by the time he looked at it from that angle again.

～

The morning of the will-reading dawned clear and bright, which seemed a good omen – or would have done so, had it not resembled exactly the weather for the past two weeks. On the upper floor of the terraced house in Farringdon, James Morgan crossed back and forth through the small dressing-room that adjoined his and Beatrice's bedrooms, seeking her opinion on this and that point of his attire. His choice of cravat, hat, and coat all presented problems. Beatrice, who had completed her toilette long before her husband, couldn't see that such choices mattered, since he would be dressed in black like everyone else, and said so.

"But, really, Beatrice," said James, staring at her. "You must see that this is an important day. And I can't very well wear the same thing I wore to the funeral. Not in front of all the Simpsons and the Lewises!"

"They'll hardly notice, dear," said Beatrice, wearily. "They'll be too busy thinking about themselves, and what they're going to get, to pay any attention to you or what you have on."

As it turned out, she was half right, for when the Morgans arrived at the parlour in Mrs Simpson's house, they were only spared a few glances from the company already assembled there. A fire had been lit in the grate, and with the windows firmly shut, the room was sweltering. Several chairs had been brought in from other parts of the house and arranged in a row facing a low table, behind which the lawyer Mr Perry stood. He, like most of the occupants of the chairs, was sweating profusely. But the attention of the assorted relatives and in-laws of Mrs Simpson was drawn not to their own discomfort or anticipation; rather, it centred on the two ladies seated in the front row of chairs. One was the silvery-haired Mrs Russell, Mrs Simpson's mother-in-law; sitting beside her was a lady whom Beatrice had never seen before. By leaning to the right and peering around Miss Simpson in a rather undignified way, Beatrice concluded that the mysterious lady was somewhere in her thirties, and almost certainly not English.

"Something in the way she holds herself," she whispered in the ear of James, who was anxiously awaiting her report, "and the way she's dressed – you can tell..."

But she did not get any further in her description, for the opening of the parlour door distracted them both and sent a general murmur around the room. Ned Hyland entered in a travelling coat, mouthing a word of apology to his uncle, who nodded gravely and gestured to him to sit.

"What is *he* doing here?" James hissed. Beatrice, watching as Ned took a seat at the far edge of the last row of chairs, shook her head to indicate that she did not know. She let her eyes linger on Ned for a moment, but, though she felt sure he must have sensed her gaze, he did not look her way. Beatrice turned back around in her seat.

James reached for Beatrice as Mr Perry began the preamble of the will. Beatrice registered the pressure of her husband's hand on her arm with a flash of surprise, and saw, with a sidelong glance at him, his hopeful smile. It had been a long time since James had touched her so deliberately; indeed, it had been a long time since *anyone* had... but then she remembered Ned Hyland taking her hand in Hampstead Heath, and cut off that last thought. She told herself that the flush spreading through her cheeks was just the result of that ridiculous fire; the servants, apparently intent on honouring Mrs Simpson's preferences even after her death, had built it too high.

The servants were now being named in the legacies read by Mr Perry. After them came a few of the Lewises, and then Miss Simpson, who dabbed her eyes with a handkerchief as the solicitor named the sum of five thousand pounds. Then, the slightest hint of emotion penetrated Mr Perry's monotone as he read out, "'To Master Ned Hyland, I leave my copy of *Oliver Twist*, which I know to be his favourite of Mr Dickens' many excellent works.'"

Beatrice glanced around instinctively at Ned, but he had lowered his head so that she could not see his reaction. Beside her, Mr Morgan had squeezed his eyes shut in evident relief, and a couple of the Lewis cousins who had already received their legacies looked as though they were unsure whether or not they should laugh.

"'And the residue of my estate'," Mr Perry read out, "'I leave to Miss Rose De Mille.'"

There was a brief, shocked silence, following which the room broke out into a confused chatter. It was clear enough that the younger lady by Mrs Russell's side must be Miss De Mille, since there was no one else in the room who could fit that name – but now another question had emerged: who *was* she? Who was this interloper who had replaced Miss Smith in Mrs Simpson's good graces, and how had she managed to do so? Beatrice suddenly felt herself the recipient of many looks, some triumphant, some curious, some sympathetic. Though the announcement had made her stomach lurch, she had managed to keep her composure, sustained by one last hope: the codicil, which Ned had told her about a fortnight ago.

Mr Perry called for silence, and as soon as it was restored, informed those assembled of the existence of said codicil. "This addition to Mrs Simpson's original will is as follows: 'to Mrs Beatrice Morgan, I leave the sum of a hundred pounds.'"

Beatrice heard her husband's furious intake of breath; she heard the burst of noise as everyone in the room started talking again, this time unrestrained in expressing their curiosity and wonder, for Mr Perry was replacing his papers in his valise and had evidently concluded his duties as executor. But these sounds came to her only distantly, drowned out by the loudest sound of all: the shouting that had started up in her own brain. She watched, and gave a faint shake of her head, as James got up from his seat and strode forward to confront Mr Perry. She tried to rise from her chair to stop him from disgracing himself, and her – but instead of gaining a standing position, her legs buckled, and she would have fallen had a pair of sturdy arms not come around her, steadying her with a grip on both her elbows.

"Come on," said Ned Hyland, shifting one hand from Beatrice's elbow to her shoulder as he half-turned her in the direction of the door. "You need to get out of here."

∽

Just as night had always seemed to fall more quickly on the house in Highgate than anywhere else, so too did the change of seasons. Yesterday had been the last day of August, but already brown leaves had formed a layer on the driveway, and golden leaves were spinning through the air, though there seemed to be no breeze to move them. One of these golden leaves landed in Beatrice's dark hair; Ned brushed at it ineffectually and then lowered his hand as soon as he realised what he was doing. Beatrice did not appear to have noticed the touch. Breathing heavily, she said, "I think I'm going to be sick."

Ned halted them at once and put a light hand to Beatrice's back. "You'd better try, then," he told her. She let her head droop, and the leaf fell out of her hair of its own accord. As her breathing hitched, Ned felt justified in what he did next: untying her bonnet strings and removing the weight of that headgear from her neck, then gently gathering a few loose strands of her hair, tucking them behind her ears and securing them with a hand at the nape of her neck. Her skin felt hot to the touch, so hot that Ned began to feel a little worried.

"It's no wonder you feel sick after sitting in that room," he said. "The only wonder is that more people don't feel the same. If..."

Beatrice made a noise to indicate that he should stop talking, but then, a moment later, lifted her head again, dislodging Ned's hand. "I don't think I'm going to be sick after all. But I think I'd like to sit down."

Ned nodded, and turned his head this way and that, looking up and down the drive. "I don't see any benches. We'd better go back to the house..."

"No! No." Beatrice clutched at his arm with both hands to stop him moving. "Never mind. Let's stay here for a minute, and I'm sure I'll feel better." A minute later, though, she groaned, and Ned shifted his position, afraid that she was going to be sick again. But the groan soon formed into words. "Oh, God." Now Beatrice was holding onto him so tightly that it almost hurt. "Oh, God, Ned, what am I going to do?"

Ned drew in a deep breath, and sighed it out through his nose. "I don't know," he told her.

"It's a joke," Beatrice said, her voice a little muffled now, for she had inclined her head towards Ned's shoulder as though to hide her face in his coat sleeve.

"She did like her jokes," Ned said grimly, but regretted the words an instant later when Beatrice lifted her head and fixed her hopeful gaze on his face.

"Then you think it can't be true? You think she must have left me something more, after all?"

"That wasn't what I meant," Ned said, wincing. He forced himself to meet Beatrice's gaze. "I mean – she has treated you very badly. Giving you only enough to pay back your husband's debt." Another groan sounded deep in Beatrice's throat, like that of a wounded animal. "And giving her estate to this stranger, when everyone expected it would be you – I think that might be a special kind of joke. The kind only she would think of."

Beatrice was still gazing at him, but did not seem to be really seeing him at all as she went on, "Ned, tell me what did I ever do to her? What have I done to deserve this? Why is she punishing me?"

"I don't think it's anything you did," Ned said helplessly.

"Maybe she always meant to give her money to this stranger…"

"And the house."

"… and the house, too, and she just let the others think otherwise by paying attention to you."

"But then why would she tell me –" Beatrice broke off. Ned, turning her bonnet in his hands, turned more fully to look at her.

"Did she ever tell you that she meant you as her heiress?"

"Not in so many words, no. But everyone said so…" Beatrice stopped again, loosening her grip on Ned's arm as she thought hard. "And she didn't contradict them. And you saw it yourself in the way she treated me – different from those others who were always hanging around her. It – it was always understood that – if I married well…" She stopped for a second time. The colour drained from her face as she met Ned's gaze, her eyelashes trembling. "You don't think…?"

Before she could finish her sentence, a voice echoed across the drive, and they both looked back to see that Mr Morgan had left the house, and was advancing towards them, calling as he went, "Beatrice!" Ned felt Beatrice stiffen, but he kept hold of her all the same, not sure yet if she was steady enough to stand by herself.

"Beatrice," Morgan said again, drawing up level with them. He seemed incapable of saying anything else: his face was flushed, blue eyes bright with anger, and a rivulet of sweat was making its way down his temple.

"She's not feeling very well," Ned said, and Morgan's eyes flashed towards him.

"Yes, thank you, I can see that for myself." Reaching for Beatrice, he locked an arm around her shoulders as Ned reluctantly let her go, and faced them towards the gate. But swinging back at the last minute to face Ned, Morgan said, "When you go back in there, you can tell your blackguard uncle that he hasn't seen the last of me. I *will* fight this to the end."

"How can you fight it?" Beatrice exclaimed. "It's what she decided. It's not Mr Perry's fault..."

"Don't you defend him! There's something wrong, I know there is. Something's been hidden, or kept back – something's due to us, and we'll get it!" Morgan raised his voice, and now it was Beatrice tugging him on towards the gate. He walked backwards for a moment, his eyes still fixed on Ned. "You'll see – we'll get it!"

It was only when they had disappeared that Ned realised he was still holding Beatrice's bonnet in his hands.

6

A STRANGE CASE

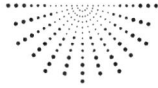

r Perry was of far too calm a disposition to rant or rave the way another man might have done, after being confronted with such unwarranted hostility merely for doing his job. But that afternoon, returning from the will-reading at Highgate, was the closest Ned had ever come to seeing his uncle rattled. Mr Perry kept reaching for his cravat to straighten it compulsively, and he became fixated on a loose thread in the sleeve of his black frock coat. "That man," he said a few times, as the carriage jolted them to and fro, and then finally he held out his sleeve for Ned's inspection. "He has torn it, don't you think?"

Ned had not told his uncle about the threat Mr Morgan had made to him on the drive: it did not seem necessary, considering how disturbing Mr Perry found it already that the man had seen fit to confront him in the parlour after the reading. "It only looks like a loose thread," Ned said, but his answer did not seem to comfort his uncle. Leaning back against his seat, Mr Perry sighed.

"You weren't there. When that man Morgan came up to me – and shouted at me, like a savage – and even put hands on me! In front of all those people."

"I'm sorry," said Ned. In truth, he could only muster a vague sympathy for his uncle, Beatrice's shock and despair still being at the forefront of his mind. Her plaintive questions seemed to sound in his ear over and over. *What have I done to deserve this? Why is she punishing me?*

"I have met many strange people and seen many strange things in my line of work, Edward, I can tell you, but never in my life – never before have I – today – and when I was just discharging the orders of another – disrespecting the dead, but of course it is the dead who leave us to arrange their business – clean up their messes…" As his exclamations became more and more disjointed, they seemed less and less intended for Ned's ears, and he felt justified in letting his attention drift away once more. It was therefore some time before he realised that Mr Perry had asked him a question.

"Yes – sorry, uncle, what did you say?"

"I asked: what time is your train home?"

When Ned told him that his train was at six, Mr Perry sighed again and did not speak for the rest of the cab journey. Back in his office, Ned handed him Beatrice's bonnet, which he had forgotten to give back to her. "I don't suppose you'll want to risk going to their lodgings and seeing Mr Morgan again," he said, "but maybe you could leave it in the house in Highgate, where she can come to collect it?"

Mr Perry looked down at the bonnet distractedly, and then put a hand to his forehead. He frowned as though he had a headache.

"Are you quite well, uncle?" Ned asked, finally beginning to feel the stirrings of alarm. "Mr Morgan seems to have shaken you. Maybe you should lie down..."

"It's not just that man," said Mr Perry, shaking his head. "No, Edward, this has been a strange case, from beginning to end. I don't mean the will itself – that is explained easily enough, at least..." Meeting Ned's questioning look, "... at least, when you know the particulars. No, I mean the people surrounding it, the *characters*, shall we say: all those people who were there today, and then, of course, the one person who was *not* – Mrs Simpson herself..."

"I think I know what you mean," Ned said slowly. His uncle lowered his hand from his forehead, and seemed to struggle for speech for a moment. At length he said,

"I don't like to ask this – and of course, your mother and father will be expecting you home. But I feel that, for once, for this evening, at least, I would prefer not to be alone. It's not that I have any fear of that man Morgan returning – no, not at all. It is just that with this case, this strange case, there are some things weighing on my mind, and though I can't see how I could have done things any differently, I should like to..." Mr Perry trailed off and paused, looking to Ned as though for guidance. Then, looking down at the bonnet in his hand, he seemed to be struck by something. "And as for you – well. You must be looking for answers too, mustn't you? If not for yourself, then on Mrs Morgan's behalf."

The expression on Mr Perry's face now made Ned feel that his uncle had guessed much about how Ned felt about Beatrice, even if he had never seemed to see any of it. Caught off guard by his penetration, Ned took a moment to respond. "You want me to stay in London tonight? I suppose I can. If I write to Mum and Dad now, they might be worried for a little while but will have word by morning."

"Yes," said Mr Perry, in evident relief, "Yes, very sensible, Edward. You do that now." He watched anxiously as his nephew walked to the desk and composed a hasty letter. When it was finished, he held out a hand for the envelope. "Let's post that right away. And then..." Casting an eye around the dark office, with an expression resembling distaste, which Ned had never before seen on his uncle's face in relation to his surroundings, "Then let's go somewhere else to talk."

~

Beatrice was not in any position to reflect on the details of her conversation with Ned as soon as she got home. There was too much happening around her, with James having worked himself, by now, into a high state of excitement. He vacillated from resentful mutterings to lamentations of despair to outright vengeful declarations, pacing the small space of their apartment, ripping from himself the cravat and jacket whose choice had given him such trouble that very same morning. Then he began to dash off letters – lots of hasty, ill-written letters, to his creditors, to old friends and comrades-at-arms and family members. Since last week, he had incurred more gambling debts: to which neither he nor Beatrice had given much thought, given that they had counted on receiving a sizeable legacy today.

Beatrice watched from over his shoulder, issuing a sympathetic word or a gentle remonstrance here and there. At length, once James had come back from posting the letters, she managed to persuade him to sit for a little while in their small dining room, where she had heated up some leftovers from the day before. Beatrice's cooking was not always satisfactory, especially on the second day of consumption, but this time James ate it without complaint. His walk to the post office seemed to have siphoned off some of his excess energy, and though he still chewed with a vigour that was not exactly necessary, his eyes were trained on the far wall of the dining room rather than roving in their sockets, as they had been.

"What a joke," he said, at length, and Beatrice started, for it was the very same word that she and Ned had used to describe the day's events. "What a joke, her leaving everything to the French girl."

There was something in the familiar disgust of his tone that made Beatrice sit up in her seat. "Do you know her? Miss De Mille?"

James's shake of the head made her sag back in disappointment. But then, swallowing his mouthful of hard potato, he said, "I don't know her. I know *of* her." Meeting Beatrice's gaze, "She's Mr Russell's natural daughter."

"His –" Beatrice stopped, staring at him. "But Mr Russell is dead."

"Yes, he is." James wiped his mouth with his napkin and stretched out his legs under the table, paying no heed when they struck Beatrice's own feet. "And *when* he died – twenty-odd years ago – he wasn't living with Mrs Simpson but in France with his mistress. There's something the old lady never told you, I imagine. I was only a boy when it happened, and my mother told me the story."

Beatrice shook her head fervently. "She always talked about him so fondly – her Theo – never talked about her second husband at all."

"Yes, you'd swear Andrew Simpson was the one who'd betrayed her. But he was a dull dog: it would never have occurred to him to betray anyone. No, I suppose the old lady preferred Mr Russell because he was more interesting." James rose to his feet and began to move around the table, with some of his former agitated energy. "*That* I can understand, but leaving everything to his daughter with that other woman? Her idea of a joke, you may be sure. And the joke was on us: who else? We're the ones who put up with her, worked for her, and helped her. Of course we're the ones she would ignore, at the end of it all."

"She didn't ignore Eliza Simpson," Beatrice pointed out, and James halted in his pacing for a moment.

"Yes, that's true enough. And after Eliza being the one who spread all that scandal about you last winter... well, I suppose it must have been me and you she didn't like, then." Concluding his reflections with a shrug, James wandered out of the room.

"Do you really think she didn't like me?" Beatrice demanded, following him through her bedroom and into the adjoining dressing-room. James cast a sympathetic look at her as he began to unbutton his shirt. She pursued, "Do you think I was... a disappointment to her, somehow?"

"Have you got a clean shirt for me?" James said in response, and Beatrice nodded, going out to the ironing board in the kitchen, where she had folded some of her husband's clothes the evening before. When she came back to the dressing-room, he took the shirt from her hands and looked at her considering for a moment, before putting his arms through the sleeves.

"If the old lady *had* liked you," he said to her, almost gently, "do you really think she would have only left you a hundred pounds?"

Beatrice was silenced. James gave her shoulder a comforting pat before side-stepping her and going to the wardrobe. He took out an evening coat and shook out the fabric. "I'll be at my club. And *you'd* better get some rest. No need to wait up for me like you did last time."

"Very well," said Beatrice, vaguely, and tilted her head very slightly in response to the kiss he planted on her cheek: her mind was already far away.

∾

Ned was surprised at the place that Mr Perry chose for their discussion – a hot, crowded tavern on the South Bank – was more surprised still when his uncle greeted the waiter by name and ordered two pints of bitter for them.

"I haven't come here in quite some time," his uncle informed him, "but they remember me." He reached for his drink as the waiter set it down, and then, seeing Ned's hesitation, "What – not used to it?"

"I've drunk before," Ned confessed, regarding the amount of liquid in his glass, "but not this much."

"Well, tonight you can make an exception, just as I am doing. Have you ever seen me drinking before?"

"No," Ned said.

"No, and you're not likely to again." Mr Perry took a long sip of his beer and then leaned back in his seat. They had chosen a table in the corner, beside a window overlooking the Thames. The London sky was streaked with orange and gold, and low on the horizon, the sun was a heavy red orb, its colour broken up into fragments in the shifting waters of the river. "Well," said Mr Perry, at length. "Where shall I begin? I first began to work for Mr Andrew Simpson not long after his marriage to Arabella Russell, in 1825. I had only just opened my own practice back then. Mr Simpson was in debt, and his marriage to then Mrs Russell helped him out of it. She had accrued quite a fortune from her first husband: in fact, Mr Russell had left her with a great deal more than expected. He also left a handsome settlement for his daughter..."

"His *daughter*?" Ned repeated.

"Yes, Miss De Mille, whom you saw today. Well, I suppose I had better explain that too."

The sun had disappeared on the horizon, leaving only a faint red outline around the brown rooftops, by the time Mr Perry finished relating the story of Mr Russell's abandonment of his wife. Ned was utterly silent as his uncle talked of Arabella Russell's determination to stay on in her marital home and her insistence on maintaining the fiction that her husband had gone abroad for "business" – until Mr Russell's death, a mere year after he had left England to live with his French mistress, had made the maintenance of that fiction no longer necessary. A year later, Mrs Russell had become Mrs Simpson, and moved to the house in Highgate.

Listening to all this, Ned began to feel that he understood something more of Mrs Simpson's character. He thought of the look that he had sometimes observed in her eyes: a look as though there was nothing in the world that could surprise or disappoint her anymore. Her first husband's betrayal, as well as wounding her, must have been a great blow to her pride. Yet, instead of crumbling, she had made her own version of the truth and stuck to it. Ned imagined that most of her relatives and hangers-on must have known the true story – no doubt it had added to Miss Simpson's rancour in hearing "Theo" constantly praised while her more virtuous brother was ignored – but he had never heard a whisper of it, and he was sure that Beatrice had not, either.

"What about Beatrice?" he asked his uncle. Their glasses were now empty before them, but the waiter had not strayed into their corner of the tavern for some time, perhaps because he had noticed they were in close discussion with one another. "Did Mrs Simpson really never intend to leave her anything? Why adopt her in the first place if she was not going to provide for her?"

"I don't understand why Mrs Simpson adopted that little girl," said Mr Perry, after a long pause. "It was shortly after Mr Simpson's death: I was executor of his will, too, and at the reading was the first time I saw Beatrice. Mrs Simpson had named her, clothed her, given her a home: of course the speculation began then, among all her cousins and in-laws, that Beatrice would be the one to inherit her estate. Only *I* knew the truth: that Mrs Simpson had already decided on her heir years before. And it was to be Miss De Mille."

"She had decided even back then?" Ned said, in disbelief.

Mr Perry nodded. "She came to me a few years after she and Mr Simpson were married. I believe it was a visit from the child that decided her – a visit from the child in France, who came with her nurse to visit Mrs Simpson in London. The child's mother stayed behind – wisely, I should say. The child was said to resemble Mr Russell in many respects. Mrs Simpson informed me, not long after little Miss De Mille had returned to France, that although she was aware that the child would already receive a settlement from her father, Mrs Simpson wished to provide for her, too. In case she and Mr Simpson had no children – which they did not – and in case her husband died before her – which he *did* – Mrs Simpson decided that she wanted Miss De Mille to inherit the house."

Ned was silent for a minute or two, taking this in. "But Miss De Mille didn't *need* it," he said in a low voice. "Not like Beatrice did."

"Perhaps not back then," his uncle said, musingly. "But Miss De Mille's mother – Mr Russell's mistress – was a woman with expensive tastes, you see. Mr Russell's settlement on his daughter was meant to be given over to her once she came of age, or married. Unfortunately the settlement was placed in the care of the child's mother, and over the years following his death, she spent it all. When *she* died last winter, she left Miss De Mille with nothing. Miss De Mille came to England to live with her grandmother, Mrs Russell..."

"That old woman who was at Beatrice's coming-out party," Ned exclaimed.

"Yes, the very same. When Mrs Simpson heard of Miss De Mille's difficulties, she wrote to Mrs Russell to assure that her granddaughter would be provided for. Rather, *I* wrote to Mrs Russell on Mrs Simpson's behalf – Mrs Simpson wished to keep a distance from her first husband's relations. But Mrs Russell heard that Mrs Simpson's ward was to celebrate her coming-out, and showed up at the party, I believe, to thank Mrs Simpson in person."

"Another?" said the waiter, who had come to clear their

empty glasses. Mr Perry, with a glance up, shook his head and thanked him.

"So Miss De Mille *did* need the inheritance, in the end," Ned said slowly. "But that doesn't change the fact that, all along, Mrs Simpson had no intention of giving Beatrice anything. Had she?"

Mr Perry shook his head. "Until the codicil of a hundred pounds was added a few weeks ago, there was no mention of Miss Smith – I mean, Mrs Morgan – in the will."

"And the hundred pounds was only to pay back Mr Morgan's debt," Ned said bitterly.

"Was it, indeed?" His uncle shook his head, turning to gaze out at the river. "After what I witnessed today, I would not be surprised at all to learn that Mr Morgan has made many enemies."

"He only married Beatrice because he thought she would inherit," Ned said, his own anger and disbelief now loosening his tongue. "And Mrs Simpson *knew* this – knew that Morgan was wrong, and let it all happen anyway. What do you think Mr Morgan is going to do, now that he's sure Beatrice will never get anything?"

"I don't presume to know," said Mr Perry, sighing, "but I *do* know that marriage is a bond more easily made than it is broken. He made a vow to be with Beatrice, for richer and for poorer, and now he is obliged to stay by her side regardless of these new circumstances."

Ned blew out his breath. He rubbed his forehead with his hand and glanced out the window. Darkness was rapidly falling. Suddenly he wanted nothing more than to be in bed, nestled in blankets and forgetful, for a time, of all that he had just learnt. Mr Perry had not ordered them another round of drinks, which must mean that he was getting ready to go, too: Ned was about to suggest that they get moving when his uncle spoke up again.

"Everything that I have told you so far about this case, everything I have done in the service of Mrs Simpson, and her husband before her, all fell within the bounds of my own profession, and while I sometimes privately questioned certain details – Mrs Simpson's adoption of Beatrice, for instance – I never had any scruples as to the rectitude of my own actions." Mr Perry lowered his gaze to the table, scraping at the wood with a fingernail. "That was, until Martha Grant wrote a letter to Mrs Simpson."

"Martha Grant?" Ned repeated.

"Beatrice's aunt," Mr Perry told him, smoothing the table surface with his hand, as though to make amends for the minor damage he had wreaked to it moments before. "Beatrice had told Mrs Simpson, when she first found her, that this aunt had taken care of her for some years after her parents' deaths before abandoning her."

"Her parents died?" Ned frowned. "But Beatrice told me they had abandoned her."

"It was her aunt and not her parents who abandoned her. Or so we thought, until Miss Grant's letter told us otherwise. According to this woman, Beatrice was not abandoned by her but ran away of her own accord. The name of Miss Grant's niece was Felicity: hearing that Mrs Simpson had adopted a girl found in the Southgate graveyard where Felicity's parents were buried, and named her Beatrice, Miss Grant was able to put two and two together. She wrote to Mrs Simpson thanking her for taking the child in and asking to meet her. Mrs Simpson showed the letter to me, and asked that I handle the affair on her behalf."

Ned felt as though cold fingers had just pressed against his neck. "And so you... handled it?"

"At Mrs Simpson's suggestion, I wrote to Miss Grant telling her that the child in question had died of cholera. There had been an outbreak the year before in London – in 1848. Many of its victims had been buried in mass graves: by including Beatrice in their number, there was no way that Miss Grant could verify what I told her."

"Uncle..." Ned breathed. "Why would you do such a thing? How could you tell a lie like that?"

"My own reasons were straightforward enough." Mr Perry was still avoiding his gaze. "I needed money at the time, and Mrs Simpson was willing to pay me handsomely in exchange for writing one letter – to a woman who, in any case, would not be able to provide for Beatrice as well as Mrs Simpson could."

"But she was her family," Ned exclaimed. "Nothing can replace that. And Mrs Simpson *didn't* provide for Beatrice in the end. She brought her up to be a lady and then – and then, nothing."

"I assumed, as I think many people did, that Beatrice, given her advantages, would marry well. As for Mrs Simpson, no doubt she came to the same conclusion as me: that the child would be better off with *her* than with her aunt."

"She had no right to decide that." Ned rose to his feet, the movement sudden and almost unconscious.

"Where are you going, Edward?" Mr Perry asked, looking up at him at last.

Ned looked back at him uncertainly, and then forced himself to speak. "I'm going to tell Beatrice the truth."

"Wait just a moment –"

"I don't care about professional secrets, or confidences, or any of what you're about to say. Enough has been kept from her all her life: she deserves to know!" Ned had raised his voice, and a couple of people in the tavern were looking their way. Mr Perry got to his feet, and reached out, stopping Ned with a hand to his arm.

"You are right – absolutely right. She does deserve to know. But it is too late in the day now for you to go and see her. In the morning, you may go and tell her everything I have just told you." As Ned continued to hesitate, Mr Perry pressed on, "Facts won't change overnight. And for you to go marching off to Farringdon now would be asking for trouble. Her husband..."

"I'm not afraid of him," Ned said.

"You ought to be. *I* was, today." Mr Perry kept his gaze fixed on his nephew. "I am as anxious as you are for Beatrice to know the truth – and to know my part in it, too. When you tell her, you must leave nothing out. Only that way can I begin to make amends. But you must go when you are less likely to be interrupted: you must allow time for what will be a long and painful narrative." He sighed and drew back, casting his eyes around the crowded tavern. "As I have done."

"All right," said Ned, reluctantly. "I'll wait till tomorrow."

∽

Beatrice's memories of the time before Mrs Simpson had found her might have been distant, but there was one thing that stood out among them, whose sting Beatrice still felt years later: duty. Her aunt Martha, who had cared for Beatrice from the time that her parents had died of smallpox (which had happened when Beatrice had been only a year old), had always made it clear to the child that she was doing so only out of duty. Aunt Martha had made sure that Beatrice knew, at every turn, just how detestable a duty it was, to be saddled with her care. She counted up every expense she had incurred in her new role as guardian, and complained of her to neighbours and friends, not caring whether or not Beatrice was within earshot.

Her name had not been Beatrice back then, but Felicity. The name meant 'happiness'; she had looked it up once in the dictionary and could hardly believe it. Whenever the name 'Felicity' rang out in Aunt Martha's sharp, grating tones, Beatrice found herself hating it more and more. And so, on the day she met Mrs Simpson and her whole life changed, she did not let that name escape her lips. She let her new mother choose her name. 'Beatrice' seemed more elegant, anyway, and more in keeping with her new life.

Under Aunt Martha's care, Beatrice had dreamt for a long time of what it would be like to have a loving mother. When Mrs Simpson took her in, she knew that she had found it. Rather than regarding her presence as a headache, or counting the various costs of keeping her, Mrs Simpson seemed to see Beatrice as a pleasant addition to her drawing room. "Isn't she delightful?" she would say to the servants, when Beatrice was banging on the piano or splashing paints around on an easel. She asked Beatrice her opinion on things – on books they read together, on people who came to visit the house, on events that were going on in the world outside – and listened to the child's answers, as though they meant something.

And though Beatrice knew that Mrs Simpson, like Aunt Martha, had counted every penny she spent (her savings on candles being an example of this), no mention was ever made of the expense to which the upkeep of a child must be putting her. From engaging music and art teachers right up until dressing her for her coming-out, Mrs Simpson had provided Beatrice with everything she needed to make a dazzling debut in society.

Beatrice, standing in front of the wardrobe in the dressing-room of the apartment in Farringdon, gazed now at these coming-out clothes, most of which had never served their original purpose. The white organdie was still hanging on her side of the wardrobe – her husband's day coats and evening tails carefully separated on the other side. She had parted with some of her other dresses over the past few months, to pay for several unforeseen expenses, but the organdie was untouched. Reaching out to touch the delicate white ruffles, Beatrice inhaled some of the fragrance of a winter's night, when her prospects had seemed so brilliant and her world arranged just to her liking. The fragrance, trapped in the fabric until now and released into the air by the motion of her hand, brought tears to her eyes.

Beatrice felt no sense of shame or absurdity, in crying over a dress. Material objects had always held more reality for her than anything else, perhaps as the result of overhearing countless conversations on this and that cost since she was a young child. The white organdie did not just bring back to her the treasured memory of her coming-out, but the glorious lead-up to that night, too. She remembered the day that the wonderful dress had arrived, modelling it in front of the mirror in the drawing room at Highgate, glorying in Miss Simpson's palpable jealousy and Mrs Simpson's words of praise. Then there was the conversation that she and Mrs Simpson had had about the 'important opportunity' of her coming-out: a conversation whose hidden purpose had eluded her at the time, but was becoming clearer and clearer by the minute.

You must choose well, as I did, Mrs Simpson had told Beatrice during that conversation. *You must choose someone who will give you consequence, and advance you.* But Mrs Simpson, long before she had married, had already had a small fortune to her name. How could she have expected Beatrice to understand what was really at stake on the night of her coming-out, after comparing their situations in that way? Of *course* Beatrice would think of Mrs Simpson's advice as a gentle reminder to be prudent, and not as the conclusion to a years-long duty.

Taking out the white dress from the wardrobe, Beatrice carried into her room and laid it out on her bed. The apartment around her, which had been so full of noise and activity just this morning, as she and James prepared themselves for the long-awaited will-reading, was now dead silent. As Beatrice began to fold the white dress gingerly, she thought about how Aunt Martha and Mrs Simpson had not been so different after all. Both had seen Beatrice as a duty; one had merely hidden it better than the other. For Aunt Martha, she had been a burden, inherited from the deaths of her sister and brother-in-law. For Mrs Simpson, she had been – a charity case or an experiment, or perhaps both at once? Mrs Simpson had done everything she could to give Beatrice her best chance of marrying a rich husband: that had been the extent of her 'providing' for her.

The white dress folded, Beatrice returned to her wardrobe and repeated the ritual with several more dresses, placing them at last into a bandbox and sealing the lid. Then she dressed in her good blue muslin, laced up her boots and put on a light grey coat. She could not find her good bonnet, and settled for a wide-brimmed hat instead, which had the advantage of coming down low over her forehead so as to conceal some of her expression. Though she felt no shame in shedding tears of self-pity, she did not wish for any stranger to see them either.

After packing some things in a carpet bag, Beatrice was at last ready to go. She left a note for James on the kitchen table, and waited for a minute on the stairs outside their apartment, until she was sure that she could leave without her downstairs neighbours seeing. She did not know whether James would try to find her after she left, but she wanted to get a head start just in case. Bearing her carpet bag in one hand, with the bandbox stowed under her other arm, Beatrice Morgan stepped out into the nocturnal world of London.

$$\approx$$

With everything that had happened at the will-reading – Miss De Mille turning out to be Mrs Simpson's heiress, Beatrice nearly fainting, and Mr Morgan's threats – Ned had completely forgotten about his own legacy from Mrs Simpson. When Mr Perry gave him the copy of *Oliver Twist*, therefore, after their return from the tavern, he was confused for a moment. Then he handed it back to his uncle.

"I don't need it. I have one of my own, back home."

"She meant for you to have it," Mr Perry said, holding out the book again.

"She meant it as a joke. You weren't there when, long ago, she and Beatrice made fun of me for liking this book best out of all of Dickens... anyway." Ned cast the memory out of his mind with a shake of his head. "She knew I would have to come to the reading if she asked, out of respect. She knows she can carry on playing games with us just so long as we keep obeying her wishes. But I won't do it anymore."

"Or perhaps," said his uncle, "she simply saw *Oliver Twist* on her shelf and remembered that it was your favourite book, and thought you might like it after she died."

Ned gazed at Mr Perry in disbelief. "After everything we just talked about," he said, "everything you just told me, Uncle, you don't think Mrs Simpson was capable of cruelty?"

"I didn't say *that*... but being cruel to you, I don't see to what end –"

"To amuse herself!" Ned exclaimed. "What other end did she need? Leaving everything to Miss De Mille was a joke on the Lewises and the Simpsons and the Morgans, and, just the same, leaving *Oliver Twist* to me was..."

"I certainly don't think," Mr Perry interrupted, "that Mrs Simpson made Miss De Mille her heiress just to amuse herself at her relatives' expense. Bamboozling them might have been an added bonus, but her main aim –"

" – was what?" Ned prompted, for his uncle had trailed off.

"Her main aim –" Mr Perry started again, and then sighed, leaving the book down on his desk. "I confess I don't know myself. But I can hazard a guess. Though she may have been unfeeling in her behaviour towards many – towards her second husband, towards Mrs Morgan – her leaving her estate to Miss De Mille, the daughter of her rival, shows the better part of her nature: a tenderness towards her first husband, an inclination to forgive the worst parts of his conduct and an acknowledgement that his child shared no blame in the affair..."

"Unfeeling?" Ned repeated. "She wasn't just unfeeling, she was monstrous! She deceived everyone around her. You told me yourself, she had decided that Miss De Mille would inherit long before she heard that Mr Russell's legacy had been spent. And she took a child off the streets and made her into her own plaything, without any thought about how that child would grow up, what would happen to her, what chance in the world she would have once her guardian was gone..."

Ned, in his passion, had raised his voice, and he was surprised to feel Mr Perry's hand on his arm, nudging him back to reality.

"Your feelings do you credit," his uncle told him. "It *is* cruel, what has happened to Beatrice Morgan. And when you go to see her tomorrow morning, you can start to make things right. But... for the moment... you should try to calm yourself, and get some sleep."

As might have been predicted, Ned's uncle's injunction to calm down had just the opposite effect. Ned went to bed more fevered than ever, tossing and turning amid the stiff, cold bedclothes that Miss Pleasant had laid down for him earlier. Somewhere between midnight and one – he could judge the time only by the tolling of the bell in St Paul's – Ned formed the intention of burning Mrs Simpson's copy of *Oliver Twist*, and rose from bed in order to carry it out.

He found matches and a candle near his door, to light his way down the creaking stairs to Mr Perry's dark office. The book was just where his uncle had left it, amid his papers on his desk. Ned seized it up with a trembling hand. He wanted to burn away Mrs Simpson's scorn for him, venge himself on her for her cruelty to Beatrice, and purge himself of her evil presence, all at once. But as he brought the book over to the cold grate, ready to set it alight with the candle he still carried in his other hand, a folded piece of paper fell from its pages and landed on the floor.

Pausing, Ned set down his candle and bent down for the paper. He tucked the book under his arm as he unfolded the paper, and saw on it Mrs Simpson's handwriting. It was a letter – a letter to him, dated from a few weeks ago, with writing on both sides of the paper! He knew he ought to burn it too along with the book. Instead he found himself reading:

Dear Master Ned,

I was hoping to have the chance to speak to you in person, when you visited here a short time ago, but my sister-in-law tells me that you would not be persuaded to stop. She also passed on to me some other things you said, though she was too confused to be able to relate all of it: that you wished to thank me for my 'wise words' and 'generosity' last winter! Sarcasm is a tool that may be lost on the likes of Eliza Simpson, but it is not lost on me, Ned.

But let me now request, most sincerely, that you show this 'wisdom' and 'generosity' yourself in reading on just a little further, so that I might make some apology for what passed that day. I didn't send you to Beatrice with the intention of embarrassing or upsetting you. I really hoped that you would speak to her, and that she would accept you instead of my cousin. I would have preferred for Beatrice to marry money, of course, but when that was no longer possible, you, next to James Morgan, were by miles the more attractive choice. You are a good and honest young man, Ned Hyland, with enough natural talent that one day you might make something of yourself – which is more than I can say for my cousin.

I imagine that something you saw or heard that day, after I sent you to Beatrice, must have prevented you from speaking as you would otherwise have done. I know that if you had *proposed to Beatrice, she would have told me about it. I can only guess what that 'something' was. Did you see, that day, proof of what I have only recently come to realise: that Beatrice did not merely marry my cousin out of necessity, but has actually allowed herself to fall in love with him? In so doing, she has not only made herself helpless to the whims of a profligate gambler, but rendered void every lesson that I have ever taught her, about guarding her own heart and guiding herself by her own reason instead.*

In marrying you, though she did not and might never love you, she might have saved herself from the disgraceful position which she now occupies: begging me for scraps, crawling on her hands and knees just like the rest of them. And she would have found, too, as would you, Master Ned, that my generosity is not inconsiderable, so long as it is being bestowed on a worthy object. I would have made sure that you were both comfortable, and that you had the resources to help you make something of yourself.

Ned was so angry that he had to stop reading. Had Mrs Simpson thought it 'generous', to punish Beatrice for having a heart? Even if Ned had spoken to Beatrice that day, he knew that she would have turned him down: once he had seen the way she looked at Mr Morgan, there had been no doubt of that. But what if she had known that it was all a test orchestrated by Mrs Simpson – that her getting anything at all after her guardian's death would depend on her giving the right answer? Would she have chosen Ned then? Knowing that she was married to a man like Morgan was unbearable – but would Ned have borne it any better being married to Beatrice, knowing all the while that she loved another?

Only a few lines remained in the letter. Drawing in a deep breath, he determined to finish it, and held the letter at arm's length as he read on:

My doctor says it will not be long now. Of course, he has been saying that for years and here I am still. But somehow I feel that you and I will not meet again, Ned. I am sure you must be quite out of patience with me – I am sure most of my family is. Beatrice, no doubt, feels neglected too. But she has made her bed and now she must lie in it. I will not see my money frittered away by James Morgan.

I hope that this letter has made some explanation to you, Ned, for why things turned out as they did, and that if you were *angry before you started it, at least you are not quite so angry now. I wish you every success and joy in the future, and may my copy of* Oliver Twist *adorn your shelf with all your other favourites.*

Yours,

Arabella Simpson

Ned lifted the letter to eye-level, and held it so close to his candle flame that the edge of the paper began to crinkle. But he pulled it back at the last minute, prompted by the strange thought that, though he might wish to destroy it now, maybe one day the letter would be useful to him. He folded it up, following the creases in the pages, and replaced it in the middle of *Oliver Twist*. Tucking the book under his arm, he kept his candle in his other hand and ascended to his room again. It was as Mrs Simpson had written: the fury of the last few minutes had ebbed away in reading her lines, leaving only an immense weariness in its place. He blew out his candle and fell asleep as soon as his head hit the pillow.

7

A NEEDLE IN A HAYSTACK

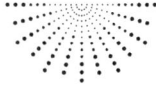

Of one thing Ned was sure – the resolution waited in his brain, ready-formed, the moment he opened his eyes the following morning: Beatrice could never be told about the contents of Mrs Simpson's letter. He had seen her confusion and despair the day before. By relating to her what Mr Perry had told him about Miss De Mille, he thought he might dispel some of that confusion: by telling her about her aunt's attempts to get in touch with Mrs Simpson, he hoped that she would not feel quite so alone in the world. But to tell Beatrice about Mrs Simpson's test would be to heap one cruelty upon another. He was sure she was already regretting her choice in Morgan; why add to her grief, and involve himself in the whole mix?

Ned had been scheduled to work in the mines this morning; as he got ready, instead, to go meet Beatrice, he spared only a brief thought for his father's anger. At any rate, his parents would have received his letter by now, and one day could not make too much of a difference. After meeting Beatrice, he would say goodbye to his uncle and get a train back to Durham; all going to plan, he would be back home by this evening. At the back of Ned's mind, too, was a little voice that wanted to tell his parents, "I told you so". They had insisted on his going to the will-reading, while he had known that to do so would be to plunge headfirst into the drama that had occupied him, on and off, for the past six years. Now that he was back in it, he would not be able to extricate himself so easily.

But as he walked through town to Farringdon, he felt none of the fear that had gripped him on the train to London the day before. He knew that what Beatrice needed now more than anything was a friend, and that was what he would be to her. There could be no danger anymore in being in her presence, even though Ned might still long for it.

Upon arriving at the address that Mr Perry had given him, Ned was told by the woman at the front door that the Morgans lived upstairs. Following her directions, he climbed a steep, narrow set of stairs and came to a door which was standing ajar. Within the apartment, he could hear heavy footsteps, evidently a man's, pacing back and forth. Growing more uncertain by the second, Ned knocked, and recoiled in alarm when the door was wrenched open almost right away by Mr Morgan.

"Oh, it's you," he said, wrinkling his nose as he looked down at Ned. "I thought she might have changed her mind and come back."

"Who?" said Ned, though of course he knew already who Morgan must mean: his heart had begun to squeeze painfully in his chest.

"My wedded wife," said Mr Morgan, "who has just left me and gone God-knows-where, with a measly note as her only explanation."

～

When Ned got back to Mr Perry's office in the late afternoon, he found that Frank Allen had been waiting for him there for some time.

"Well, well, you never told me you were back in town!" Frank exclaimed, rising from his chair to clasp Ned's hand. "I had to hear it from Miss Low, who saw you walking through Holborn this morning. Your uncle has just been telling me about the will-reading. So Mrs Morgan was really left with nothing?"

Ned nodded grimly, and turned his attention to Mr Perry as he said, "And she has just left her husband." His uncle looked up from his desk, startled.

"Left him?" repeated Frank, whose eyes were now as wide as saucers. "And gone where?"

"That's just it. We don't know." Ned briefly related to them what Mr Morgan had told him, standing at the door of the apartment – throughout the whole conversation, Ned had not been invited to step over the threshold. "She took most of her clothes, even the dresses she has not used since her coming-out – perhaps to sell them. And she left only a note, to say that she won't be coming back and not to try to look for her."

Frank gave a low whistle. "She can't have gone far," said Mr Perry. "She knows London best – I don't imagine she has ever left it before, and isn't likely to leave it now."

"Maybe she has gone back to Mrs Simpson's old house?" Frank suggested then, but Ned shook his head.

"I just went there myself. It's all shut up, with only a few servants there now, and they haven't seen anyone apart from themselves. Miss De Mille won't take possession till the end of the month."

"And why should she want to go back there, in any case," Mr Perry pointed out, "when it is no longer her own? No, there are many other places where Mrs Morgan could be. Southgate, for instance."

"The graveyard?" Ned repeated, frowning. "Where Mrs Simpson is buried? You mentioned it when you wrote to me about her funeral..."

"Not just Mrs Simpson," said Mr Perry, "but Beatrice's

parents, too. That graveyard is where Mrs Simpson first found her, on the day of Mr Simpson's funeral."

"This is the first I'm hearing about it," Ned exclaimed. "And what about Beatrice's aunt, Mary or..."

"Martha," Mr Perry corrected.

"Have you an address for her? Maybe, if Beatrice remembers the house, she might have gone back there..."

Frank, who looked like he had begun to lose the threads of the conversation, chose this moment to break in. "Pardon me," he said, as they both looked towards him questioningly. "But if there's going to be a search for Beatrice Morgan, maybe her husband is the one who should direct it."

"That might be true, if Mr Morgan was actually interested in finding Beatrice," Ned said flatly. "He told me that he has been 'so wounded' by her decision to leave, he's not sure if he even wants to see her again." Thinking of Morgan's manner as they had stood talking in the hall – his words about Beatrice spilling over with indignation rather than worry – Ned's jaw clenched. "It's an inconvenience to him, at most."

"Yes," said Mr Perry, who had begun to rummage in the drawers of his desk. "Mrs Morgan *has* been rather useful in paying back her husband's debts, after all."

"Though with Mrs Simpson dead, there's no one she can borrow from anymore," Ned said.

"What about the note?" Frank said. "Any clues in it, as to where she might have gone?"

Ned thought about it for a moment. Mr Morgan had shown him the note: it was brief, but one particular phrase had made clear Beatrice's reasons for leaving. *I have been a burden to everyone who has ever cared for me*, she had written. *I don't want to become a burden to you, too*. Ned opened his mouth and then closed it again: he felt the phrase revealed too much of Beatrice's private pain to relate it to his uncle and Frank Allen, and, in any case, it was not going to help them find her. "There was nothing," he said.

Mr Perry took out an envelope at last, and handed it across the desk to Ned, pointing to the return address that had been written on the back. "This was Martha Grant's address, when she wrote to Mrs Simpson seven years ago. I have no idea whether it is still her address today: but it is a good place to start." He hesitated for a moment, and then added, "I'm sorry."

Ned, thinking that his uncle was apologising again for hiding the truth from Beatrice, nodded resignedly. But then Mr Perry went on, "If I had let you go and see her last night, as you wanted to, perhaps none of this would have happened." As Ned stared at him, he said, "The girl doesn't have all the facts of the case. She must feel alone – friendless. If we had reached her in time..."

"It's no use thinking like that now," Frank interrupted hastily, his eyes on Ned's face, which had fallen at his uncle's words. "We'd better lose no more time, and get looking for her. Where should we start?"

~

Frank Allen was so determined to lend a hand that Ned soon gave up questioning whether or not it was right to rope him into their search for Beatrice. Mr Perry, for his part, soon gave up questioning whether or not Ned would be going back to Durham in the immediate future. What had been supposed to be a day-long trip quickly turned into a week, as with each day, new clues and possibilities seemed to yield themselves. In their first visit to the Southgate graveyard, they did not find Beatrice, or even the grave where her parents were buried, since Mrs Simpson had never told Mr Perry their names – Grant being the maiden name of Beatrice's mother, which would not be on the grave.

Next, Ned tried to track down Martha Grant at the address that Mr Perry had given him. It was in Mile End, on the other side of town, and as Ned peered up at the factory chimneys and the black canal, he wondered if this was where Beatrice had spent her early years. But the house where Martha Grant had lived was no longer occupied by her, and its new tenant did not know where she had gone: she was only able to give Ned the landlord's address so that he could make further enquiries.

Meanwhile, Frank enlisted the help of Miss Matilda Low, the daughter of the newspaper editor, who was anxious to do what she could once she heard that a friend of Ned's was missing. Together, Frank and Miss Low spent a few days visiting various boarding-houses and pawn-shops around Farringdon, inquiring at each place whether any Grants, Morgans, Smiths, Beatrices or Felicitys had passed by, in the hopes that Beatrice might have stopped there using one of those names. When Mr Low heard about this, however, he soon put a stop to it.

"What do you expect to find?" he demanded one evening, when Ned and Frank had stopped at his house after another busy day of inquiries. "You might be searching for weeks, months. It's like looking for a needle in a haystack. You two might waste your time as you like, but I won't have my daughter caught up in such foolishness."

The same thought did come to Ned in his worse moments – that they *were* looking for a needle in a haystack – but the rest of the time, he did not let himself consider it. If Beatrice was not found at the end of all this, then what awaited him? Disgrace and anger back home? No, he would not think about that possibility. They had barely started to look for her, in any case.

The next day, Ned visited the Southgate graveyard again, this time by himself, and found that fresh flowers had been placed by Mrs Simpson's grave. He plucked one, tucking it in his waistcoat pocket, and rushed right back to South Bank with the revelation fresh on his lips. But

Frank and Mr Perry were less enthused than Ned, pointing out that any number of Mrs Simpson's relatives might have left the flowers. Thus it was that Ned spent the following day tracking down every last relative of Mrs Simpson's in town, eliminating them one by one – even writing to Miss Simpson in Dover – until he could be sure that the flowers had been brought by Beatrice.

Upon hearing this confirmed, Mr Perry offered to do a round of the various flower-sellers in the vicinity of Southgate and Highgate to determine where the flowers had been bought – perhaps because years cramped in his dark office had given him an endless tolerance for tedious tasks, or perhaps because he had seen the deep shadows under his nephew's eyes. Ned was ordered to rest while his uncle carried out this task, but Ned did no such thing. Instead he left the house not long after Mr Perry himself had done so, urging Fred Collins to silence as he passed through the office. Taking a crumpled piece of paper from his pocket, which was a list made by Frank of various potential boarding-houses where Beatrice might be staying, Ned scanned the writing.

Since Frank had, by now, also been removed from their search at the insistence of Mr Low, though in his case it was to finish an article that he had been commissioned to write, Ned knew that he hadn't gotten around to all the places on the list, and set about finding the next one. He walked and walked until early evening, and by the time he returned to the office on South Bank, his lower legs were aching so intensely that he found it hard to climb the stairs.

Fred Collins had gone home by now. Mr Perry, evidently alerted to Ned's presence by the sound of his plodding footsteps, sat alone at his desk with folded arms. "Where have you been?"

"I just went to... make a few inquiries," Ned said, a little hoarsely, and came to the desk to lean a hand on its edge, because he was not sure he could stand on his own.

"I told you to rest, didn't I?"

Ned nodded and murmured his apologies, before fixing his eager gaze on his uncle. "Well? And, with the flower-sellers... did you find out which one it was?"

"I did," Mr Perry said, "and Beatrice was seen buying flowers there the other day. The flower-seller gave a perfect description of her."

Suddenly it was as if the pain in Ned's lower legs had faded into nothing. He thrust out a hand impulsively. "Thank you – thank you, uncle."

Mr Perry did not smile as he returned his nephew's handshake. "The shop is in Highgate, not far from Mrs Simpson's old house. But it doesn't tell us that much. Only that Beatrice stopped there on her way to the graveyard. She gave no name to the flower-seller, nor any other way to identify her."

"But she might go back there next week," Ned pointed out, "to leave more flowers at Mrs Simpson's grave. So we might be able to catch her in the shop or in the graveyard..."

"We can't be there at every hour of every day," Mr Perry said slowly.

"*I* can."

"Be reasonable, Edward. If someone doesn't want to be found –"

"She only *thinks* she doesn't want to be found, because she doesn't know the truth, like you said. But if I could meet her again, and tell her..."

"Edward –"

"... tell her everything, tell her that she's not alone, that her aunt tried to find her, that it wasn't her fault Mrs Simpson didn't leave her the estate, that it was never supposed to be Beatrice –" But here Ned stopped of his own accord. For though he knew that Miss De Mille had always been designated as the heir, he also knew what Mrs Simpson had written in her letter to him: that she would have left Beatrice something if she had married Ned and not Mr Morgan. Could Ned look Beatrice in the eye and tell her honestly that none of it was her fault – that Mrs Simpson *hadn't* meant to punish her in what she had done?

"Ned," said Mr Perry, and he gave a start, surprised at the sound of his nickname. His uncle had a strange expression on his face – Ned wondered if it had been there all the time since he had come into the office, and if he was only just noticing it now. "You'd better go upstairs. Your father is in the drawing room."

"My father?" Ned repeated, his alarm turning to terror as he glanced towards the stairs. "Dad never comes to London. What is he..."

"You'd better not keep him waiting any longer," said Mr Perry, and Ned, swallowing, plodded towards the stairs.

~

Mr Hyland was dressed in his Sunday best, and looked ill at ease in the small chair that he had chosen. He got to his feet as Ned entered the drawing room, and seemed disinclined to take his seat again, instead watching his son inch across the carpet.

"Why aren't you – at work?" Ned said, confused.

"I took the day off," said his father, brusquely. "Why are you moving so slowly? What's wrong with you?"

Ned explained about all the walking that he had been doing, and Mr Hyland tilted his head slightly to the side as he listened. By the expression of intense focus on his face, he looked as though he was trying hard to keep calm, but Ned could see the way his fingers kept curling and uncurling into fists at his sides.

"So *this* is what you've been doing," he concluded when Ned had stopped talking, "Traipsing around London. You know you've been gone for more than a week now? And Perry says you've got *him* joining your wild goose-chase too. What good do you hope to come out of this?"

"I want to find my friend," Ned told him, earnestly.

"Your friend." Mr Hyland ran a hand over his chin as he considered, and then glanced back at his son. "Oh, sit down, won't you? I won't have you fainting now, not till we've had it out."

Ned obeyed his father, sinking into the seat across from him. Mr Hyland, still standing, swept a glance around the room, his gaze lingering for a moment on the dark rooftops visible through the window before it returned to his son. "I gave up the day," he said. "Came all the way here, and sat here waiting for you for hours, and now I think I'll have my say." But then he paused for so long that Ned saw fit to sneak in some defence of himself first.

"I wrote you letters," he murmured, "explaining..."

"Yes, I got your letters, every one of 'em, explaining how you couldn't be dragged away, how you can't forget about this *married woman*, a woman who has upped and left her husband..."

"It's not like that," Ned insisted. "She's my friend. And she only left Mr Morgan because she knew he was expecting her to inherit – and when she didn't, she thought she must be useless to him."

"For someone who's just a friend, you know a lot about her thoughts and feelings, don't you?" Mr Hyland pointed out. "But all right, very well: it sounds like this husband of hers is a piece of work too. Still, I don't see where *you* come in. It's none of your business what they do to each other –"

"But you've got it all wrong: she hasn't done anything to him..."

"Let me finish, Ned. I told you I'd have my say and I meant it. I can only see one reason why you'd involve yourself in this whole business, and it's –" His father grimaced. " – it's that you must have told yourself you're in love with this woman, or something. Now, I don't think you know yourself what you would ever do, if this woman returned your feelings: I only *hope* that we raised you well enough to know right from wrong. But look at yourself for a minute, Ned, and ask yourself if this is wholesome? Is it healthy?"

Ned looked down at his own hands, as though they might hold the answer to his father's question.

"Your mother and I have talked about this, and we both agree we should have nipped this in the bud a long time ago. Your feelings for this girl, even before she got married, they've been pulling you away from everything that matters: from your home, your people, your work..."

"I'll go back to the mines," Ned said, "just as soon as I find Beatrice –"

"Oh, no. No, no." His father gave a bark of laughter. "That's all finished now. I can't pull any more strings for you, Ned, or make any more excuses. You've got a reputation now, see, you're 'unreliable'. Unreliable – my son!" He paused, and the disbelieving smile faded from his face. "But they're right. I don't think you mean any harm by it: I don't think you rightly see what this whole business has been doing to you. But it's been a long time since I've felt I could count on you. And you're the eldest, Ned, you're supposed to set the example for your brothers and sisters. What lesson do you think Tim will learn, when he sees you gallivanting off, shirking your responsibilities whenever it pleases you? And the girls, when they hear you're involving yourself with a married woman: what lesson do you think they'll learn about how they should behave, when they're grown up and married themselves?"

"We're not *involved*," said Ned, making no attempt to hide the despair in his voice now as he gazed up at his father. "The way you say it, it makes it sound so – sordid..."

"Isn't it?"

"No! It's pure and so is she. I know she is: I've always known. Not just beautiful, but good. No matter what she got herself mixed up in, no matter how ugly things were around her, she was never – she *will* never..." Ned corrected himself, alarmed by his own inadvertent use of the past tense. "She'll never change. And I would do anything: be her friend or her brother or whatever she needs, or go out of her life altogether, just so long as I know she's safe and..." He swallowed. "Happy."

Mr Hyland was watching Ned, his eyes full of some strange emotion – was it sorrow or pity, or both? Ned was still trying to figure it out when his father sat down at last, and steepled his hands over the join of his knees.

"And you, Ned?" he asked quietly. "Are you *safe* and *happy*? Because you don't look it to me now. You look worn out and washed out. You look like you haven't slept or eaten in a week. If your mother was here, she would be stuffing you with good food and promising that would solve all your problems: but maybe I don't have her soft heart. I look at you and all I can see is waste."

The word struck at Ned's skin and then sank right inside him, like a stone cast into a deep pool.

"You're clever," his father said. "Different. Your mother always said it – though I never saw any rhyme or reason in sending you away when you could do the same work as I do. This business of studying law – still, I would have stood back and let it happen, if you'd stuck at it: if you'd stuck at *anything*."

"I didn't like it," Ned whispered. "I didn't want to."

"Like it? Want to? And where on earth did you get this idea that the world is supposed to arrange itself around what *you* want or like? It wasn't from us, that's for sure." Resting his hands on his knees, Mr Hyland cast another glance around the room, and stopped when he saw the bookshelf. Slowly, he began to rise out of his chair. "It's that, isn't it? All those books you've always liked so much. I told your mother to nip that in the bud, too. Maybe if she had, none of this foolishness would have happened."

Ned's father's form was now half-blocking the bookshelf, but by leaning out of his chair, Ned could see that one of the books on the shelf was the copy of *Oliver Twist* that Mrs Simpson had given him. He had left it in his room the night he had found the letter, but Miss Pleasant must have brought it downstairs to the drawing room while she was tidying, thinking that this was where it belonged. Ned watched in disbelief as his father reached for the book. "No, don't..."

Mrs Simpson's letter fell from the pages, and his father stooped to pick it up.

"That was meant for me," Ned said feebly. "My eyes only." His father just snorted, walking back to the armchair as he began to read. He often murmured to himself as he went, casting occasional glances up at his son, and turning the page over only to turn it back again, as though to remind himself of some important phrase earlier in the letter. At last, folding it up again, he looked at Ned.

"So she would have left you something after all: Mrs Simpson. If you and the girl had married."

"But it was impossible," Ned said, "and you see why: she says it herself in the letter. Beatrice was, *is*, in love with –"

"You could have married money," his father interrupted. "It wouldn't have been what your mother or I wanted for you. But it would have been *something*. It would have been better than *this*." He gestured to Ned, and then rubbed at his own jacket sleeves, as though the material was slightly too tight for him.

"Better?" Ned repeated. "You say it's unwholesome – unhealthy – to love someone who doesn't love me back..."

"... no, to love a married woman..."

"... but it would be all right to *marry* someone who didn't love me back, because that makes it all respectable?"

"Marriage has a way of deciding things," his father said, shrugging his shoulders. "Maybe this girl would have come around to loving you. And having a bit of money, on top of that..."

"Always money," Ned said bitterly.

"Don't roll your eyes at me: you know it's important! And by the sounds of it, you don't have a lot at the moment. Perry had to buy you a coat when you came back from your little tour, didn't he? You were right cleaned out."

"And then I came back to Durham," Ned pointed out, "and got right back to work –"

"For a fortnight, not even..."

"I would have stayed! I wouldn't have come back to London at all if you hadn't told me to..."

"No," said Mr Hyland again, pointing at his son. "I told you to do what was right, to do your duty and no more. I thought you'd know the difference: I thought you'd have learned your lesson about getting swept up with these people. Then you never came home – your mother didn't sleep a wink that night, worried you'd had an accident on your train – and in the morning we got your letter that you'd decided to stay the night, for Uncle Perry's sake, you said, not for the girl..."

"It *was* for his sake. He asked me to stay. It wasn't until I knew Beatrice had disappeared –"

"... and I knew then," his father finished, as though he hadn't spoken. "I knew you'd fallen into the hole again: maybe you've never climbed out of it."

"You didn't want me to go to the will-reading because it was the right thing to do, did you?" Ned said, after a moment, watching his father carefully. "It was because you were hoping I'd get something in Mrs Simpson's will, just like Mum was: you just wouldn't admit it."

Mr Hyland's eyes, grey like his son's, darkened momentarily, and he leaned forward in his seat. "Turn it back around on me all you like, you young pup. But at least one of us thinks about facts, and money, and what a man is to live on besides dreams and books."

"I won't come back, then," said Ned, the words spilling out of his mouth before he could really consider them. "I'll show you I mean what I say. I'll show you I can do it myself – everything you just said."

His father leaned back in his armchair, watching Ned wearily. "All right, then. You do just that. And when you're starving and in rags in three months' time..."

"Don't come crawling to you for help," Ned finished. "Right?"

"Right," said Mr Hyland, quietly, and turned his gaze away from his son. "Well, I've said my piece. And now I'll say goodbye to Perry and go back to Durham, where I belong."

Ned, averting his gaze just as his father was doing, stayed fixed in the same position in his armchair as Mr Hyland got to his feet. He listened to the sound of his father's footsteps on the stairs, to the sound of his and Mr Perry's voices, too low for Ned to make out the words. And finally, as that sound faded too, the first tears began to fall from Ned's eyes.

∾

That night, Ned dreamt of Beatrice. He dreamt that she came to Mr Perry's drawing room and sat just in the same small armchair that Mr Hyland had occupied, listening with her hands folded in her lap while Ned described the argument that he and his father had had.

"He knows nothing about the outside world," Ned told her. "He knows nothing about anything that goes on outside of Durham. And he acts like he's the expert – like I'm the one throwing my life away when I know how to *live* in a way he never will?"

"How to live?" Beatrice repeated, thoughtfully.

"Yes, well I mean, loving you and everything else." For some reason, Ned was not embarrassed at all to admit this in front of Beatrice in his dream, and she reacted to the words with a sage nod of the head, as though it was a point that had often been discussed between them. "All its taught me, about life and the world. All I've felt. I wouldn't take it back, not for anything. But he doesn't understand that: he doesn't understand that there's anything in the world besides money and duty."

"He's like most people, then," said Beatrice, and Ned looked up at her swiftly.

"Not like you."

"You always say that." She smiled at him. "But I'm not as good as you think."

"You're better. You're everything." Ned leaned forward, wanting to reach for her, but it was as if his limbs had been locked. Beatrice watched with a light frown as he struggled against his invisible hold. "And I will find you," he managed to choke out. "I'll –" But when he repeated the phrase a second time, he found himself addressing the dark ceiling of Mr Perry's guest room. " – find you."

The picture of Beatrice in his dream had been so vivid that the next morning, he felt more hopeful than he had in a while. His father's visit, and their argument, already seemed far from his mind. When Miss Pleasant came in with a bundle of envelopes, Ned leapt for the one that had his name on the front. He tore open the envelope and pulled out the letter inside, the words on the page washing over him so quickly that he could hardly make sense of what they said at first. Then he put a hand to his forehead. He could feel a faint throbbing at his temple, and a strange whistling noise in his ears.

"Ned?" His uncle was suddenly beside him, putting a hand to his shoulder. "Ned, what is it? What does the letter say?"

"It's from the landlord of the house in Mile End where Martha Grant used to live," said Ned, a little dazed as he looked up at his uncle. "He says she died two years ago. She'll never meet Beatrice now."

8

THE WORLD OF FACTS AND MONEY

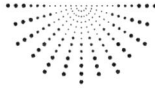

here was just one part of Beatrice's new life that recalled the old, and that was music hour at the gin-house where she now worked. It was usually at around ten in the evening, when the publicans were well-sauced but not so drunk as to become nasty or violent – that usually came later. Now that Beatrice had been working at the Princess Elizabeth for a few months, her colleagues had discovered that she could sing and play piano quite well, and at music hour she was always called upon to deliver a few performances. During those brief minutes, with her fingers moving on the piano keys and her strong voice ringing out, while bright lights illuminated the delighted faces all around her, Beatrice would feel like she had once felt as Mrs Simpson's ward: beautiful, full of promise, important.

It was always difficult to go back to the regular routine after that, to serve drinks and duck around tables and try to avoid the groping hands of the clients. It was harder still to come out into the dark once her shift was over, when all night her world had been lit by gas and filled with the warmth of many bodies. Beatrice and the other serving girls, who all had lodgings fairly near each other in Bow, tried to walk home together whenever they could. But sometimes Beatrice, sent on some task or other, like bringing empty gin barrels down to the vaults beneath the bar, or cleaning the verandah that faced onto the street, would lose track of time, and come out to find that the other girls had departed without her.

She was not as quick as the other girls, or as nimble with her hands. When the manager, Mr Wells, was not ogling her, he would berate her for her clumsiness, her tendency to daydream, or her poor memory. "You have to write it all down?" he would demand, agog, as she came away from taking an order with a notebook in her hand. "You couldn't remember what they all wanted?" When she dropped a glass, he would cry out, "Look what you're costing me!" At first she had thought he was joking, but soon she had discovered that he was not.

Beatrice's plan, when she had left her husband, had certainly not been to work in a gin-house. She had known that once the money from her dresses ran out, she would have to find some way to pay for her board, but she had been hoping to find work in a shop or something halfway respectable. Sometimes, on busy nights at the Princess Elizabeth, when Beatrice was wading through the crowd with her tray held high, she would feel as though Mrs Simpson was watching her, and shaking her head. But it was Mrs Simpson's training that had sealed her fate, that had made her unfit for any other kind of work. They would not hire her in a shop because she was too genteel. In the Princess Elizabeth, where many of the staff, including Mr Wells, put on hoity-toity airs, Beatrice at least fit in a little better, and having a pretty face could cover a multitude of sins.

Beatrice did not go out much these days. It was not just that the weather was getting colder, or that she worked such late hours in the Princess Elizabeth that she often slept half the day away. She did not want to risk meeting anyone she knew from her old life. Even in Bow, it was still possible. The danger was not so great now as it had been back in autumn, when she had first disappeared. She knew that people must have been looking for her for a little while back then, but that by now they would all have given up and forgotten.

Beatrice had hidden herself away, so successfully that she herself had started to forget that she had ever been anyone else. Her life seemed to have played out in disparate phases, with each new phase making the last seem false: the first phase as a burdensome child in her aunt's house in Mile End, not far from here; the second phase as Mrs Simpson's ward in Highgate, the longest and happiest; and this third phase, as a serving girl in the Princess Elizabeth. She wondered what other strange phases lay ahead of her, and whether other people's lives were structured in the same mixed-up way.

Losing James had hurt dreadfully at first. She knew now that he did not love her, but tearing herself away from his side when she still loved him – that had been harder than she could have imagined. It only got a bit easier once Beatrice, casting her mind back on their brief courtship, their hasty marriage and that first blissful month afterwards, began to realise that James's passion and fascination had not existed for her at all. Those feelings had been called into being because of what she represented to him: wealth and comfort and luxury. It stood to reason that, as their life grew more distant from what he had envisaged, he would start to lose interest in her. Beatrice, remembering how he had touched her arm during the will-reading, wondered how things would have gone if she had inherited. Would his passion for her have been reignited? She sometimes thought that she would have liked that, even knowing that he loved the money and not her; she sometimes felt that it would have been better than having none of him at all.

But these feelings began to fade with a little distance and time, and now, three months after she had started working at the Princess Elizabeth, Beatrice mainly thought of James Morgan with a mixture of amusement and scorn. She was sure that if she came face to face with him again, the old feelings might come back in some small measure. But they would never grip her again as they had once done. She was beginning to think that nothing would ever really grip her in the same way again.

Beatrice was grateful that the staff at the gin-house were mostly friendly. But she kept her distance from all of them, even the girls she walked home with, never accepting their invitations back to drink tea with them in their lodgings, and never inviting a single one to step over her threshold. She was not ashamed of her rented room: it was clean and respectable, but she had no desire to share the space with anyone else, even if it was just for a cup of tea.

But one of these girls was more persistent than the rest. Nelly Gale was a great admirer of Beatrice's singing and playing: her fascinated face was always one of the closest to her at music hour, and, seemingly oblivious to Mr Wells' remonstrances, she would often try to drag Beatrice into conversations while they were serving on the floor. Her nighttime invitations to tea were more frequent than those of the other girls, and she never got discouraged no matter how often she was turned down.

It was one evening, during music hour, when a brief lull had come as another performer came to replace Beatrice. Just as Beatrice was leaving the piano stool, Nelly gripped her hand and exclaimed, "You *have* to show me how to play the way you do!"

Nelly was a good deal shorter than her, and in answer, Beatrice gave her usual distant smile, gently detaching her hand. But Nelly, undeterred, followed her back to the bar, repeating her entreaties until Beatrice was forced to say something. "And how would I do that, Nelly? I don't have a piano at home."

"Neither do I," Nelly giggled, "but we can practise here."

"Wells would never let us," said Beatrice, casting a glance at the manager, who was standing near the entrance, pretending to enjoy the music while his eyes roved the room, scanning for any possible problems or threats.

"He doesn't have to know," Nelly insisted. "You know how they always keep this room open for an hour after we close? Let's practise then."

"After we close?" Beatrice was feeling tired even just thinking about it. "I don't know. I like to go home with the rest of the girls."

"What, are you scared of the dark?" At Beatrice's silence, Nelly nudged her. "Here, silly, I was just joking. I don't like walking home alone either. But we can go together, once we've finished practising."

Beatrice neither agreed nor disagreed to the plan. But, towards closing time, after she had been sent out back to clear the empty bottles, she returned to the gin-house to find, not for the first time, that the other girls had already departed for home.

Beatrice hesitated for a moment by the door that led into the main room of the gin-house. Within, the gas lights had been dimmed, and through the translucent glass pane at the top of the door she could just about make out someone sitting at the piano, whom she assumed to be Nelly. Beatrice's things were in the cloakroom, through the door just to the left of the taproom door. She could grab them and walk out into the night, and tell Nelly later that she had forgotten about their plan. Or she could stay now and teach her a few songs, and gain herself a few days of peace and quiet before Nelly started pestering her about something else.

Beatrice pushed open the door and entered the gin-house proper. Her footsteps echoed around the abandoned room as she walked towards the piano. Then, as the head on the other side of the piano turned towards her, Beatrice saw that it belonged not to Nelly Gale but to the manager, Mr Wells.

Her first thought was that he must have found out about their plan, and had come to punish them. But if so, where was Nelly? It was typical that Beatrice should be the one caught out here instead of her. Nelly struck her as one of those people who had a gift both for causing trouble, and for getting out of it.

"I thought I... left my shawl somewhere here," Beatrice began as an excuse, but Mr Wells had already gotten up from the piano and was beckoning her over.

"Come, come." He was smiling; this was a great deal worse, Beatrice found, than if he had been berating her.

"My songbird. Do you know how long I've been wanting to get you alone?"

"I must go home," Beatrice said. She had stopped in the middle of the floor, and did not move even as Wells continued to beckon her over. "I just stopped in to make sure I hadn't forgotten anything..."

"And you found me. What a happy chance!"

He must be drunk, Beatrice thought, and took a step back towards the door. "I'll be going now," she said.

"All alone? But all the other girls have already gone, didn't you know?"

"Nelly Gale said she'd walk home with me: she must be somewhere around."

"No, she's gone too," said Mr Wells, his smile broadening, and then something clicked in Beatrice's mind.

"Did she tell you she'd arranged to meet here with me? Did she –" Suddenly Beatrice was furious. "Did she arrange it so that you and I would meet here instead?"

"Oh, my dear, don't be angry." Mr Wells was moving towards her now, but at an easy, slow pace, so that Beatrice did not feel the urge to break into a run just yet. "I had to take my chance, and Nelly was kind enough to oblige. You won't begrudge us that, will you?" Now he was a few mere paces from her, and reached for her hand, holding it firmly even as Beatrice tried to pull back. "Such soft hands: lady's hands. That accent of yours, too – you're so different from the other girls who work here." He stepped even closer, lowering his voice. "Is that why I can't get you out of my head?"

"You tricked me to get me here," snapped Beatrice.

"And you turned me down, so we're fair and square." Mr Wells put his hands on the light cotton dress she wore for work, getting a firm grip on her waist before pulling her towards him. "But you won't deny me this time, Beatrice. Here we are, with no one to disturb us. I don't see how you can have any objections. I know I may seem severe sometimes, when this place is busy. But I promise you, I can be gentle, too, given the right occasion and the right... encouragement..." He raised a hand to the top of her bodice, and Beatrice slapped it away.

The look of intense focus on Mr Wells's face was replaced by one of intense confusion. "What –"

"You will not touch me," Beatrice hissed, summoning every ounce of venom into her voice that she could, and forcing herself to meet his gaze, to glare him down. Slowly, she watched her manager's face turn red.

"You're not so high and mighty, Beatrice Smith," he exclaimed. "You're working here, after all, what do you expect? Sooner or later..."

"I do not expect *that*," Beatrice said, taking one step back and then another. "Not now and not ever."

"Then you're fooling yourself," said Mr Wells. "You're not in a convent, Miss Smith; you're in a place where people like to enjoy themselves – to enjoy good drink and good women. And you can't really think people are going to ignore you, looking the way you do. Do you know how many times I've protected you from clients who would have tried to keep you here after hours, or followed you home? They would have paid me well, too, if I'd turned a blind eye. But I told them, 'She's a good girl.' And I do think you're good, Beatrice – very good..."

He had started to move towards her again. Beatrice bolted for the door, hearing his furious voice behind her. "Women like you don't hold all the cards, you know! We have some say in what you do, too! And I can make you sorry for what you've done tonight, Beatrice Smith!"

"You'll never make me sorry," Beatrice shot over her shoulder, and raced out into the night. The solitary walk home held no terrors for her, after that; her veins were buzzing with adrenaline from her near-escape, and the rest of her body tensed up in anger at the deception that had been practised upon her. But the following evening, when she showed up at the Princess Elizabeth, ready to give Nelly Gale a piece of her mind, Mr Wells informed her that she had been dismissed.

∾

Ned's mad quest had finally ground to a halt with the discovery of Martha Grant's death, and, with the few months of calm that had followed, he was able to look back now and see that the others were right: it had been a wild goose-chase. Even if they had had more to go on than a bunch of flowers, a forgotten grave and a house in Mile End, was it even possible to rescue someone who didn't want to be rescued? He really believed now that Beatrice had willfully disappeared, and could only hope that, wherever she had conjured herself to, she was at least safe. ('Happy' seemed too tall an order these days.)

Despite this realisation, Ned had not spoken to his father since his visit to London. His mother wrote from Durham a couple of times a week, always to say some variation on the same thing: to tell Ned that his father was out of sorts, and plead with him to come back and make things right with him. Ned, for his part, always gave the same response: that he would come back to Durham just as soon as he felt welcome there. It would take his father's assurance, as well as his mother's, to convince him of that – and so far he had heard nothing.

But while Mr Hyland might have been right about the wild goose-chase, his prediction about Ned had not come true. Three months had passed, and Ned was neither starving nor in rags, even though he hadn't had a penny from Mr Perry, his parents or even Mr Low's newspaper.

What he was, however, was bone-tired. Clerical work might not have been as physically taxing as going down into the mine, but it took its toll all the same. Ned worked in one cubicle among several others, in the large, airless office of an insurance company in Camberwell. He worked every day except for Sunday, with a half-day on Saturday. On full days, he sat in his cubicle from eight to half past six, with only a half hour to go outside and sit in one of the nearby eating houses. No one spoke in the office of Simms and Parkinson's except for the secretary, and the secretary only spoke to issue instructions.

Ned remembered, as a young boy, watching Mr Perry, and thinking about how he would give anything not to end up in such a dull profession. How was it that, in trying to avoid one, he had ended up in another a great deal worse? The work at Simms and Parkinson's was beyond tedious: preparing receipts and recording payments.

"So it hasn't killed you yet!" announced Frank Allen with forced cheerfulness one Sunday afternoon, when he and Matilda Low dropped in on Ned in his lodgings. He was quartered in a boarding house just up from Simms and Parkinson's, along with several other clerks from the same company, but none of them ever chatted even when they passed each other in the corridors.

"No," Ned agreed, stifling a yawn as he poured some tea for his guests. They were in the dingy visitors' parlour on the ground floor, and the landlady had brought out a tray five minutes ago.

"Father was wondering when you might have the time to work on something for our newspaper," said Miss Low, eyeing Ned carefully.

"I never have time for anything anymore," Ned admitted, sitting in the chair across from her. "Except working."

"But this shouldn't be too much of a challenge," she persisted. "It's about clerical work, so you wouldn't have to interview anyone, just write about your own experiences. At this time of year, when so many clerks are forced by their employers to work, if not Christmas Day, then every other day around it..."

"I'd like to help," Ned told her. "Really I would. But it's been so long since I wrote something. Besides, I do so much of it at work already – though that is writing of a different kind."

Miss Low fell silent. With an anxious glance at her, Frank said, "Anyway, that's not why we came. We've heard something, Ned, about James Morgan. It seems he wants to divorce Beatrice, on the grounds of abandonment."

"Divorce her?" Ned repeated. "Why? All that scandal and expense..."

"The scandal will hurt her more than it hurts him. As for the expense, I daresay he'll manage it in the long run." At Ned's questioning look, Frank looked pained. "He wants to marry again – and for money, this time."

"I shouldn't be surprised," sighed Ned. "Who's the lucky girl?"

"It's Mrs Simpson's sister-in-law, the one who always used to hang around the house in Highgate." As Ned's jaw dropped, Frank smiled sympathetically. "Miss Eliza Simpson."

"She – and *him* – what?"

"Well, she's got money now. Five thousand pounds."

"And I doubt she's had any other offers," added Miss Low.

Ned shook his head as he tried to take it all in. "But..."

"We went to see your uncle before we came to you," Frank said. "He knows the solicitor Morgan has hired. Perry says, if this divorce can be turned into an annulment, it will be far less damaging to Beatrice if she ever comes back. He thinks it's likely to be done, since this solicitor in particular is very correct, and doubts can be raised about the wedding ceremony: the small number of witnesses, for instance, Beatrice's young age, and the possibility that she was coerced into the ceremony."

Ned was silent for a minute or two, considering this. He had not seen his uncle since he had moved to his boarding house. Mr Perry wrote him occasional notes with updates on the search for Beatrice, but nothing substantial had come to light. The flowers had stopped appearing in the Southgate graveyard, which indicated either that Beatrice had left London, or that she no longer had money to be buying flowers. Ned hoped – with what little energy for hoping he had left – that it was the latter, because if she had really left London, then they had very little chance of finding her again.

"It will be better for Beatrice," he said at last. "Whatever can be done to save her reputation – should be done."

Frank and Miss Low exchanged a glance. "If Morgan can be convinced of it, too," said Frank, "then it will be full steam ahead. Perry thinks you're the best person to do it."

"Me?" Ned repeated. "Then he must be out of his mind. I'm the last person to be able to convince Mr Morgan of anything."

"You care about Beatrice," said Miss Low after a moment. "Everyone can see it. And if he has any compassion left for his wife, then you might be the one to bring it out."

"You're hoping to appeal to his better nature," said Ned, scornfully, "but I'm telling you, there isn't one."

"Then appeal to his sense of practicality instead," Frank exclaimed. "Remind him that an annulment is less complicated than a divorce. The man likes to act hard done by – suggest that he and Beatrice were both ill-used by Mrs Simpson. He married her on false pretences, and she was pushed into it. Use whatever arguments you like, whatever you think will make the man tick. But, for God's sake, Ned..." Frank grimaced. "Whatever else you do, you can't give up now."

"I gave up a long time ago," Ned informed him.

"So you don't love her anymore, then?" Frank said, his voice harsh.

"Whether I do or not," Ned evaded, "it's got little to do with anything. I've got to live in the real world now: the world of facts and... and money and..." Aware that he was quoting his father, he trailed off lamely.

"Right," Frank said after a moment, with a glance at Miss Low. "And this isn't a real problem?"

"I just... can't do the things I used to do anymore," Ned explained. "It's nothing against you."

Miss Low murmured something about the room being too warm, and got up to leave. When the door closed behind her, Frank leaned forward in his chair. "She's been a brick, you know," he said. "The least you could do is thank her."

"Thank her?" said Ned, confused. "I'm grateful – grateful to you both for still carrying on with this. But I don't see..."

"She's always been fond of you," Frank continued. "You *must* know it. But she kept back only because of Beatrice. And now you're saying you don't care about Beatrice anymore, that you'll drop the whole thing..."

"I never said I didn't care." Ned's mind was reeling.

Glancing at the door, he lowered his voice. "But – you mean, Miss Low was fond of me in... *that* way?"

"Still is," Frank replied with a sigh. "Which doesn't give other fellows much of a look-in." He eyed Ned in disbelief. "You really didn't know?"

Ned shook his head, and Frank leaned back again in his chair.

"Well," he said at length, "so you're living in the world of 'facts' and 'money' now."

Ned gave a faint smile. "It didn't sound as stupid when my father said it."

"No, I suppose not. Fathers have a way of making anything sound impressive." Frank joined his hands, twiddling his thumbs. "But seeing as it's Saturday, and your half day off anyway, do you think you can leave the world of facts and money for a little while and go visit Mr Morgan?"

"I'm pretty sure he lives in that world, too," Ned pointed out. He looked at Frank for a moment. "But I suppose I can go see him. I suppose there's not much harm it can do now."

~

Before he went to see Mr Morgan, Ned stopped at his uncle's office. He was relieved to find that Mr Perry had stepped out for a few minutes, leaving only Fred Collins at his stool. Ever since getting the bad news about Martha Grant, Ned hadn't felt the same about his uncle. Colluding with Mrs Simpson to keep Beatrice from learning the truth had been one thing when her aunt was still alive, and when there had still been some chance of the relationship being salvaged if both parties learned about each other. But now that Beatrice's aunt was dead, a door had been closed, and knowing that his uncle had helped to close it changed things.

Ned's business in South Bank was the work of a few minutes. He ascended the stairs to the drawing room, found the copy of *Oliver Twist* in the exact spot on the shelf where his father had replaced it a few months ago, and drew from it Mrs Simpson's letter. Descending once more to the office, he kept up an easy conversation with Fred while he threw the letter into the grate, and watched the flames curl over Mrs Simpson's handwriting until it had faded away.

If Beatrice was to have any chance at an annulment, Ned had decided that any evidence to the contrary, such as that contained in Mrs Simpson's letter, had to be destroyed. Ned knew that Beatrice had been pushed to marry Mr Morgan, even if she had loved him – even if she did still love him. It couldn't have been what she had planned for herself. But a stranger reading Mrs Simpson's letter, to Ned, would be able to argue that Beatrice had had the luxury of choice.

Any stranger, it struck Ned, who happened upon their little drama now without the context of the last ten – twenty – thirty years, without knowing all the players, alive and dead, might come away from it with a very different picture of reality. He remembered how his father had made it all sound so sordid, as though Beatrice and James Morgan were equally degenerate, and as though Ned had been pursuing Beatrice to seduce her away from her husband. If he knew now what Ned was about to do – try to persuade Mr Morgan to get an annulment from his wife – probably he would think even worse of him. But his father, despite his professed love for facts, did not possess all of them in this case.

At the house in Farringdon, Ned was informed by the downstairs neighbour that Mr Morgan was at Miss Simpson's new house in Fulham. He trooped across town again as the sun began to lower in the sky, and was surprised to find, at the address the neighbour had told him, a bustle of activity. A cart was parked on the pavement outside the house, which stood a little way back from the street, and men were unloading boxes and carrying them inside. Behind the cart was a carriage, which was also being unloaded of various paraphernalia; Ned glimpsed Mr Morgan carrying a mirror that was almost as tall as he was.

At the centre of it all, though taking no part in the proceedings herself, was Miss Eliza Simpson. She looked radiantly happy as she gave orders here and there, admonishing the delivery men for letting a shelf brush against the coat of new paint on the front door, or for carrying a case of crystal-ware like it was a sack of potatoes. When she recognised Ned, her face lit up even more, and she called out, "Well, if it isn't Mr Hyland! James, dear, just look who it is!"

Mr Morgan, who had just emerged from the front door empty-handed, mopped the sweat from his brow and grimaced towards Ned. Miss Simpson advanced towards the new arrival excitedly, holding out her hand. "You heard our news?"

"Congratulations," said Ned weakly, his gaze fixed on the sapphire set in the ring on Miss Simpson's finger, as he wondered whether Mr Morgan had bought it on credit or asked his new fiancée to pay for it out of her own pocket.

"We decided to get moving and organise some of James's things, though of course we will have to wait a little while before the wedding. I have bought a few new things, too..." Nodding to the cart, "Nothing extravagant, just a few little things to put around the place." They watched as one of the men buckled under the weight of an elegant writing-desk, before getting his grip on the item again. "My house is still new, you see," Miss Simpson continued, "and I want to make it feel more like a home."

"You have sold the house in Dover?"

Miss Simpson nodded with a smile. "And now I can live in London just as I've always wanted – with the most charming of husbands." She raised her voice on this last part, and Mr Morgan, now heaving a portmanteau towards the front door, sent a weak smile in her direction. Miss Simpson turned back towards Ned. "Of course, I really shouldn't talk like this. It's quite scandalous." Lowering her voice, "Because until the divorce is settled, we're not even officially engaged. James's solicitor says there is such a lot of paperwork to sign, and they haven't even started! Oh, how my heart sank when I heard that. I thought a case like this should have been clear-cut enough. She left him, after all, without a word..."

"She left a note," Ned corrected.

"She left him without a word," Miss Simpson continued, as though he had not spoken, "which is abandonment – breach of promise..."

"Hyland," said Mr Morgan, emerging from the front door for a second time. "Are you going to stand around there or help us?"

"James is just being funny," said Miss Simpson, watching as her fiancée moved towards the open door of the carriage. "But you'd better go, all the same."

Ned, accordingly, spent the next half hour lifting boxes and pieces of furniture, until sweat was running down his face and long-forgotten muscles were aching. He tried a few times to open a conversation with Morgan, who was either genuinely absorbed by his task or pretending not to hear him, but at last, when they were lifting chairs into the drawing room, he found his opportunity.

"So you're trying to divorce Beatrice."

Mr Morgan, who had crossed the room to check the curtain rail inside the window, half-turned at the question. "Trying? Oh, I'll manage it, all right. But I don't see what business it is of yours, Hyland."

"It isn't, of course," said Ned. "I'm just surprised you're making it so hard for yourself. An annulment would be quicker, easier."

"You need certain conditions for an annulment," Mr Morgan said, turning fully now and folding his arms. "Non-consummation, for one thing. And, well..." A nasty smile overspread his face, "I'm afraid Beatrice and I don't qualify on that front."

Ned ignored the jibe, though he could feel the heat rising to his face. "Non-consummation isn't the only condition. There are other factors, too – which, in the case of your marriage, might give you a case for annulment." He recited the same list that Frank had told him.

Mr Morgan looked thoughtful now. "So, you say, we could both claim we were coerced?"

"It's possible," Ned said. "And with an annulment being so much quicker than a divorce, in a few months' time you could marry Miss Simpson. She seems... reluctant to delay."

"Yes, well," said Mr Morgan, "She's not getting any younger."

"What are you two men talking about?" said Miss Simpson, entering the drawing room with a quick, bouncing step only to pause by one of the boxes Ned had put down. "But this isn't supposed to go here, is it? No, these are things for the bedroom. I'll just check..." She opened the box and began rummaging for a minute. "Yes, none of these things belong here."

"I can bring them up," Ned offered. "If you show me..."

But Miss Simpson ignored him. She had just pulled out something silver, something which caught the last gleams of sunlight pouring through the window. Wordlessly, she rose to her feet and held it up for Mr Morgan's examination.

"What is this doing here?"

"I don't know," he said, taking a few steps towards her to look more closely. "I've never seen..."

"It's hers! I've seen it around her neck a hundred times. Didn't I tell you to get rid of all her things? And didn't you say you had?"

"I *did*, dearest," Mr Morgan said, with a placating gesture, "but it must have gotten mixed up with my things somehow. I didn't see..."

"You didn't *see* a silver locket? No, you kept it to remember her by, didn't you? You couldn't get rid of it! You still love her!"

Miss Simpson had gone red in the face. Mr Morgan, shaking his head, still had his hands held up in a placating gesture as he approached her. "I never loved her, dearest. I was taken in by her once, that's all. But now I couldn't care less about her..."

"It's true," Ned couldn't resist adding; Miss Simpson half-turned towards him. "He didn't even try to look for her when she disappeared."

"Stay out of this, Hyland," said Mr Morgan, without looking at him. "Eliza, dear, give me that locket and we'll get rid of it now. You'll never have to look at it again, I promise..."

"You promise?" she said, in a small voice.

"I promise." He had reached her now, and, prying the locket from her hands, tossed it aside so that it landed with a *clunk* on the floor. As Mr Morgan began to kiss his new fiancée, Ned picked up the locket from the floor and discreetly took his leave.

He did not open it at first. It felt like a violation of Beatrice's privacy, to pry into something that had hung close to her heart for so long. But when she disappeared, she must have left it behind for a reason. Was it something she wished to forget? Once he got back to his room in

Camberwell, Ned opened the locket, and saw the miniature inside of a couple: well-dressed, the woman with dark hair just like Beatrice's. As his heart skipped a beat, he realised that he had never really given up looking for Beatrice. He had just been waiting for the next lead.

∾

After Beatrice was dismissed from the gin-house, it was not long before she had to leave her room in Bow. The rent was due the following week, and as Beatrice had only received some of her wages for the previous month, she could not pay it in full. She pleaded with the landlady, who was sympathetic but firm: so many other working girls were looking for a room to stay in that she could not afford to accommodate a girl who was not.

Beatrice packed up various things: willow-patterned plates and an Oriental rug and the china shepherdess that had stood on the mantlepiece, and many more little treasures that she had bought to make her room cosier. Over the next week, these treasures ended up being sold off one by one, to pay for her board. She stayed in a different place every night, always seeking somewhere cheaper. But between her meals and board, it all began to add up. She had not been saving for the past month. She had had no idea of having anything to save *for*.

One day, Beatrice went back to the Princess Elizabeth, showing up outside the gin-house at the time when she knew most people would be starting their shifts. She watched from the street as the girls, some familiar, some unfamiliar, filed in through the main door, turning left for the cloakroom. They were all too absorbed in their chatter to notice her: all except for Nelly Gale, who, perhaps sensing the force of Beatrice's glare on the back of her neck, swung around and did a double-take when she saw her.

"Beatrice Smith, is that you?"

"You know very well it's me," Beatrice said, marching forward to tower over the girl. "And I want you to clean up the mess you've made."

"You don't look well," Nelly lamented, looking her up and down. "Have you been sleeping at all? And your clothes..."

"You're to tell Mr Wells to give me my old job back," Beatrice said.

"I could no more tell him *that* than I could fly!" Nelly tittered, and then sobered up again at the expression on Beatrice's face. "I'm sorry, dear, it *is* too bad. But you know how he is. When one of the girls gives him cheek..."

"Is that how he's telling it?" Beatrice said, with a bitter smile. "That I gave him cheek?"

"I really should go." Nelly glanced behind her, at the main entrance, which stood open after the passage of the most recent girl, and the door to the cloakroom beyond it. "I'm going to be late..."

"You're not going anywhere," Beatrice snapped, "until you do something about this! Look at me! I can barely afford to keep a roof over my own head now. This is your doing, Nelly Gale, and you've got to fix things before it's too late!"

"What can I do, Beatrice?" Nelly smiled helplessly. "I don't have any money to lend you. I can't talk to Mr Wells. I can't put you up in my own room – my landlady would find out and put me out on the streets."

"You can't," Beatrice said, "or won't. It all comes down to the same thing. You've ruined me."

What Nelly Gale said next surprised her. "You've ruined yourself, Beatrice Smith. Girls like you always do. You tease all the men until they're out of patience with you. But you're not so pure and good – everyone knows it. They say you were married before and your husband threw you out on the streets..."

Beatrice lunged for the other girl. What happened next seemed like a bad dream. She had barely given Nelly a few shakes when the girl started screaming at the top of her lungs, and then Mr Wells showed up, dragging Beatrice and calling her a string of bad names – and then the police showed up. By now, most of the staff of the gin-house had gathered outside to see what was going on. As Beatrice was led away, she felt all their eyes on her, but it was not their disapproval that stung the most: it was the strong sense that came to her, not for the first time, that Mrs

Simpson was watching from somewhere, shaking her head, and murmuring, *I knew it.*

She spent the night in the police station, and the following morning returned to the boarding house where she had been staying to find that her room had been given away in her absence, and stripped of her remaining possessions.

It was now a week from Christmas, and Beatrice knew that her priority, more so than getting a hot meal, was to find somewhere to sleep. She wandered and wandered, getting farther and farther from Bow and into a part of the city that she had never seen before. As the snow began to fall, Beatrice was glad that she had not yet pawned off her gloves or shawl. Her boots were good, too, letting in a bit of water but staying mostly dry.

But it was getting dark, and she still hadn't found anywhere to sleep. All the boarding houses she passed were too expensive for the few coins she had in her pockets. She thought of the people from her past – Mr Perry, Ned Hyland, Eliza Simpson, even James. Pride had kept her away from them all this time. But now she would have been glad of their helping hand, if she'd had any idea how to get to them from where she was. The few strangers who passed her on the street looked too frightening to ask for directions. And it was dark, getting darker by the minute.

With every step she took, Beatrice was remembering more and more clearly how it had felt after she had run away from Aunt Martha's house. The elation that had died down to be replaced with despair. The gnawing cold, like now, as she had wandered the streets. The people who had taken pity on her – fewer now than there had been then, for she was a grown woman. And the church door, then as now, looming up before her. It was not the same church where she had taken refuge back then. But it might as well have been, for the relief with which Beatrice threw herself at its door – only to find the handle, when she turned it, firmly locked.

There was no one around her: not a living soul that Beatrice could see, and no sounds but the whistle of wind and the whirl of snowflakes. Her hand still on the locked door handle, she felt herself sink to the ground. Cold and damp seeped into her dress and then her underskirt: it was uncomfortable at first, but after a time, as her whole body adjusted to the temperature, it felt quite comfortable. Beatrice's hand let go of the door handle, and she felt herself slip further and further, until she was lying on the ground.

The world looked different from this angle. The distant, bobbing lights of nearby streets, and the occasional flitting shadow, were the only signs of life that she observed. As though chased away by the emptiness, she thought she could see her own life ebbing away, contained in the mist of each breath that rose before her before dissolving into the night. The edges of her mind were beginning to blur, and when she slept at last, it was just another gentle step downwards into the dark. She did not see where she was being led, and did not think it mattered much anymore.

$$\approx$$

Ned could not throw off his responsibilities now with the careless abandon that he had shown before, in searching for Beatrice. But he began to spend all of his breaks, instead of sitting in an eating-house waiting for his food to be cooked, pursuing his new and crucial lead. He bargained with colleagues, swapping hours here and there to try to get earlier shifts, meaning that he would finish in time to be able to look around town before nightfall.

He knew that there was no point in tracing the locket – it was probably a family heirloom. But there was the miniature of Beatrice's parents inside: if he could trace the artist, he could trace the parents. Ned set about his quest, this time around not feeling at all like he was looking for a needle in a haystack. There could only be so many artists around town who painted family miniatures. He visited workshop after workshop, but as each day passed with no new discoveries, he did not despair. When he got his half-day on Saturday, he changed tack, and enlisted Frank and Miss Low's help in searching through old newspapers from the late 1830s, the time in which he judged it most likely that Beatrice's parents had died.

The three of them pored over articles and obituary announcements in the library, and it was Miss Low who finally hit on a likely one, just as they were all ready to drop. "Look! 1838, Jenny and Hugo Grey of East Barnet, died of smallpox. Survived by their daughter Felicity."

"Does it say the mother's maiden name?" Ned said, leaning over her shoulder, and when his eyes landed on 'Grant', his breath whooshed out of his lungs. "That's it. That's them. I've found them!" He took out the locket, which he had been carrying in his pocket all this time, and opened it to look at the faces of the couple in the miniature.

Frank and Miss Low, though happy to have helped, did not see, as Ned did, the all-important nature of the revelation. So it was alone that he went to Southgate graveyard the following afternoon, under a white sky swelling with clouds. Loose flakes of snow were drifting on currents of air rather than falling straight down, and he rubbed at his coat as he passed through the gate into the graveyard.

He checked Mrs Simpson's grave first, as he always did, and felt the familiar twinge of disappointment when he saw no flowers there. Then, lowering his head as he felt the wind begin to pick up, he turned down an aisle and began to search, among the various inscriptions, for the names of Jenny and Hugo Grey.

Stories burst upon him with each grave he passed. Some were freshly dug, with new, marble headstones; some were so old that lichen had obscured whatever inscription had once been carved into the stone.

He had nearly reached the far wall of the graveyard when at last he found them. Their headstone was modest, and rotting leaves and petals had gathered over the writing, where someone – Martha Grant, perhaps – had left flowers a few years ago and never had the chance to clear them away. Ned did so now, taking off his glove and carefully sweeping the stuff away, wincing whenever his bare fingers made contact with the frozen ground. When that was done, he took out the locket, the silver cold in his palm, and opened it to look at the miniature, glancing from it back up to the names on the headstone, and then down again, as though hoping that one might verify the other.

Finally he spoke. "Mr and Mrs Grey." His voice rang out, too loud in the silent graveyard. "I promise you that I will find your daughter."

He heard the wind moan as if in answer, the creak of the tree branches seeming to want to drown out his resolution. He spoke it again. "I will find her. I *will* find Felicity."

All at once the wind dropped; the trees became still again, and where Ned had felt alone just a moment before, he suddenly felt the opposite. Looking all around him, he seemed to see the crowd of headstones as if it were a crowd of people, all waiting to watch what he would do. Ned scrambled to his feet.

The sunset must have happened sometime in the last few minutes, but it had been so totally obscured by the white clouds overhead that the ambient light had simply turned from white to grey. In this grey light, Ned fled, tripping over the uneven ground and not wanting to look down, fearing that he may have stepped on someone's grave. He thought he could hear voices, now, a low murmur, even though the place was empty. Then, turning his head to the right, he caught a flash of movement between the headstones, and looked straight ahead again.

If I don't look, Ned told himself. *It's not real.* And he had made it all the way to the gate with this logic, and had his hand on the latch, when he realised that the strange, low murmur was gone, and in its place was the soft sound of crying.

Ned stood still for a minute or two, working up his courage before he made himself turn back. He walked back a little way, towards where he had seen the movement, and turned in that direction. It struck him as a strange coincidence that Mrs Simpson's grave should also lie this way – and then the coincidence became a miracle, as he came within sight of the headstone and saw Beatrice Morgan kneeling before it.

To have reached the end of his quest so quietly and abruptly was not something that Ned could ever have imagined. So as he stood there looking at Beatrice in amazement, he could not believe, at first, that she was real. His eyes noted none of the real details of her appearance: the fact that her dress was torn and stained, that her dark hair was tangled and unkempt, that, as she knelt on the frozen ground, she was shivering violently. The idea of her had been so strong in his mind, for these last few months, that for the moment it predominated over the reality.

Then despair and worry rushed in to replace his ecstasy in seeing her, as he saw all of these things at once, and, on top of it, that she was crying. Ned came forward and knelt beside her. Beatrice glanced at him, startled. The cold seeped into his kneecaps, but he did his best to ignore it, reaching out tentatively, so as not to alarm her further. When she saw what he meant, she gripped his hand with both her own, so tightly that he thought she might crush his fingers. Looking down, he saw that her fingernails were torn and covered with dirt and blood.

"Ned," Beatrice said, after a minute or two, still gazing at the headstone in front of her. Her voice was so hoarse and reedy that the moan of the wind nearly drowned it out. "Are you really here?"

"I was just asking myself the same question about you." Ned glanced down at his nearly-crushed fingers, and gave a half-smile. "But not anymore."

The night that she had fallen down by the church door, she might have died if not for the minister who had found her a few hours later. He had come to check that the front door, the door where Beatrice lay, was locked, and instead found her. Beatrice had woken from sweet darkness to cold, harsh reality, but the minister guided her with his arm and with his words, bringing her around the side of the church to another door.

"This door is never locked, like the other one," he told her. "Our church is always welcome to those seeking shelter. If you had gone only a few steps further, you would have found it."

That was just typical of her kind of thick-headedness, Beatrice reflected, and she thanked him, curling up in a pew. He brought her a blanket and then left her in peace, but all night the chattering of Beatrice's own teeth kept her from drifting fully into sleep.

The next morning, she woke up to find the minister sitting near her pew. He asked her when the last time she had eaten a hot meal had been, and when she told him that it had been days, maybe a week, he reached into his pocket for a pen and paper and wrote something down. Passing it to Beatrice, he said, "Go to this address, and they will take care of you. It's not far from here."

Beatrice was relieved to find that he was right: the place was not far. She found herself in a large hall, where she stood in line behind others who looked even more miserable and cold than she felt, while workers behind a counter ladled out some kind of stew. When it was Beatrice's turn to be served, she had to stop herself from wolfing it down, walking a few feet to a table first and sitting down before she dug in.

The hot meal brought alive some of her deadened senses. She thought of last night, and of what would have happened if the minister hadn't found her. How could she have lain down and given up so easily? She was not a coward; she was not weak. But last night she had felt both; she had nearly let herself fall into oblivion.

That evening, she waited until the service in the church was over, and found the same minister who had helped her. He walked down the stairs from the pulpit, and they sat together in one of the pews. He was not much older than her, and something about his earnest eyes reminded her of Ned Hyland, so Beatrice found herself telling him about last night, and how she had wanted to let herself drift into darkness.

"And you don't believe in God, you say," the minister said, once Beatrice had finished talking.

"No," she said.

"But you felt all the same that, to surrender as you nearly did last night would have been to throw your life away."

"Of course," Beatrice said, shrugging her shoulders. "I can't know everything that's going to happen, or what good I might be to someone, or what purpose my life might serve later on. Just because it serves no earthly purpose now, doesn't mean it will be like that forever."

"What you're talking of is a kind of plan: a plan for your life, and the life of many others, that you will never understand in its completeness."

"Exactly," said Beatrice, and the minister turned towards her.

"Well, what is that *plan* if not God?"

That night, she slept in the church again, but the following morning, when the minister asked her if she would be going to the soup-kitchen again, she shook her head. "I have something else to do first." She hesitated, and then told him, "It's my birthday today."

"Your birthday!"

"Well, not my real birthday. One that was chosen for me. But it's all that I've got."

"A chosen birthday is certainly better than no birthday at all."

"Exactly." Beatrice asked him for directions to Southgate graveyard, and he wrote them on a piece of paper for her, just as he had done for the soup kitchen. Then, handing the paper to her, he eyed her doubtfully.

"It's a long walk."

"I have all day," Beatrice assured him.

The walk *was* long. It brought her in and out of the city, through patches of countryside, and frequently Beatrice had to lean against a wall or gate to gather her strength. By the time she got to Southgate, a light snowfall had begun, and the graveyard was deserted. She followed the familiar path to Mrs Simpson's grave, her scuffed and sagging boots struggling over the uneven ground. As she knelt by the headstone, she saw, in her mind's eye, Mrs Simpson shaking her head again. Suddenly Beatrice found herself saying out loud, angrily,

"Stop that!"

Stop what? Mrs Simpson spoke to her in that flat, amused tone that she had always reserved for people she considered beneath her: Ned and Eliza Simpson and the like, but never Beatrice – until now.

"You know very well what I mean," Beatrice said, her voice slightly unsteady. "Looking at me the way you're looking at me now, as if I had any other choice than to be what I've become, as if *you* left me with any other choice..."

I left you with plenty of choices, Mrs Simpson's voice replied, confident and unrepentant. *I gave you every opportunity. Is it my fault that you threw them all away? Your little indiscretion at your coming-out party, that ended up costing you so much...*

"It cost *too* much," Beatrice said, passionately. "It was more than I deserved. I was – stupid and vain, I can see that now, but you always taught me to pay attention to how I looked, and to notice what effect I had on other people..."

So the sins of the child are always to be thrown back upon the mother. But I am not your mother, Beatrice, and never claimed to be.

"You're the only mother I remember," Beatrice insisted. Then, at the sound of footsteps, she looked around.

There's someone here! came Mrs Simpson's voice in her head. *Be quiet for a moment.*

Obedient as always, Beatrice kept her mouth shut and waited as the footsteps sounded closer – and closer – the wind picked up her shawl and flapped it about, and she struggled to bring it back under control. The footsteps got quieter again, and, peering over the headstones, Beatrice saw the back of a man's head, moving towards the gate.

Stop that snivelling, Mrs Simpson's voice admonished her, and, raising a hand to her own cheek, Beatrice was surprised to find it wet with salty tears.

"I didn't mean to..."

You know I hate such displays.

"I know. I'm sorry. I'll try to..." But Beatrice dissolved into tears again before she could even finish pronouncing the words, and she felt Mrs Simpson's presence recoil in disgust.

When Ned Hyland came to kneel beside her, Beatrice wondered if it could be another conjuring of her imagination. Mrs Simpson's voice had felt as powerful as though she had really been beside her. Could Beatrice's mind have put together such a picture of Ned Hyland, whom she hadn't seen for months, who looked skinnier and paler and more weary than he had ever been before?

"Ned," Beatrice said at last, coming right out with it. "Are you really here?"

"I was just asking myself the same question about you." Ned looked down at their joined hands, and out of the corner of her eye she saw him smile. "But not anymore."

She was glad he was here, glad he was real, and glad she had something to hold onto. She said as much, and then added, "I was just talking to Mrs Simpson."

"Talking to her?" Ned sounded alarmed. "Was that what I heard?"

"Yes, we were having an argument. She says I threw away all my opportunities – that I deserved to be disgraced, that I deserve to be in the state I am now."

"That's not true," Ned said, crowding up closer to her so that they were shoulder to shoulder, "And anyway, Beatrice, you know it was just in your head."

"I know, of course." She sighed. "But still it feels real. She's a part of me: a part of how I think and act and feel."

"She's not the only part of you." Ned sounded eager, even excited now. "There's your family, too – your aunt Martha..."

"I hope *she's* not a part of me," Beatrice said grimly. Ned stopped short for a moment, before going on,

"And your parents. I found their grave just now, Beatrice."

"Did you?" she said, mildly interested. "You know I've forgotten their names. How terrible."

"Their names were Hugo and Jenny Grey," Ned said fervently. "And they loved you. They even had this made for you – look." He drew out the locket and opened it so that Beatrice could see the miniature inside. "You left this behind, when you ran away."

"I didn't see any need to bring it. What good is it to carry around a picture of people you don't even remember?"

"Because they're your family. Because they'd like to be remembered."

"*I'd* like to be remembered. Doesn't mean anyone will remember me."

Beatrice sensed Ned turn towards her. "*I'll* remember you," he promised. "All my life." She smiled at him in vague thanks.

The snow was falling more thickly now, coming to rest on the joins of the crosses and pile around the headstones in drifts. Ned looked around. "We should get out of here," he said, tugging at Beatrice's hand. "This hill is too exposed. Come back to Mr Perry's with me. We have so much to talk about, so much to tell you..."

"I'm not going back with you, Ned," she said, and his grip on her hand slackened for a minute.

"But you have to. You can't carry on alone like this, like you have been... I've been so worried about you, these past few months. I've sometimes been afraid I'd never see you again. Now that I've found you, I... I can't..."

Pathetic, said Mrs Simpson's voice in Beatrice's head, and she gave a start. *Listen to him, whining and wheedling, thinking that because you're so low now, he finally has a chance with you. This is all he's wanted for years. He couldn't be happier to see you weak and miserable like this.*

"Beatrice?" Ned was pressing her hand again. "Did you hear any of what I just said?"

She blinked at him, and shook her head apologetically.

"She's talking to you again, isn't she," said Ned, his gaze now straying past Beatrice, as though Mrs Simpson stood just at her shoulder. "Why are you still listening to her?"

"She said she was never my mother," said Beatrice, "but I wanted her to be."

I thought I taught you better than that, scolded Mrs Simpson. *Never to need anyone: to stand on your own two feet. Look at that man beside you now, on his knees, begging for just a sliver of your attention. Look at him, and tell me that love isn't weakness.*

"What's she saying now?" Ned said urgently.

"She's saying that... love is weakness."

"Well, she's a hypocrite. Did you know that, Beatrice? Did you know that, in the end, she blamed you for the same weakness she had herself?"

Beatrice's attention was at last caught fully by Ned's words. She turned towards him. "No, I suppose you didn't," he said, sighing. "She didn't punish you in her will because you married Mr Morgan – no, she could see that you didn't have much of a choice there. She blamed you because you fell in love with him. Because you took on his debt as if it was your own. And yet, why do you think she left all her money and estate to Miss De Mille?"

Mrs Simpson was silent in Beatrice's head. Ned went on, "Because she loved Mr Russell, her first husband, enough to forgive his betrayal, enough to make his child her heir."

And what about your *love, young man?* taunted Mrs Simpson's voice. *Your all-consuming love, that made you keep coming back for more, coming back to seek out my ward again, even as you got hurt and disappointed each time? Next to your excesses, the rest of us look positively reasonable.*

Beatrice began to turn away from Ned again, but he caught her shoulder, saying again, with even more urgency than before, "What? Does she say now?"

"She's saying," said Beatrice, without looking at him, "that you love me. And that it made you a bigger fool than the rest of us."

Ned kept a hold of her shoulder as he said, "Yes, she's right. I love you. I love you so much that you can throw any insult you want at me, it won't stick. You could ignore me for a whole year and, at the end of it, I'd still be happy if you looked at me for just a single second. I love you and I don't care if it makes me weak or foolish or forgetful of other important things. And I don't care if you marry someone else and spend the rest of your life with him, happy, I'll still love you and I'll still be your friend, if you want me to. And I don't care what *she* has to say about it."

Ned let go of Beatrice's shoulder and got to his feet. "She wanted me to propose to you, back then," he said, and Beatrice stared up at him. "After your coming-out party. She thought I would have been the better choice than Morgan. But I didn't say anything, because I saw you looked happy with him." He looked down at Beatrice. "To have you, possess you, no matter what way you felt about it: maybe it would make me happy for a little while. But you'd hate me for trapping you. And sooner or later, I'd hate you for not loving me back. No, I prefer things the way they are. Having you here with me, having found you again: that's more than enough for me."

Ned raised his voice again, addressing the swirling snow now, his voice echoing around the empty graveyard. "Do you hear me? It's enough, it's all over, and you're to leave us all alone now. We don't want to see or hear from you again, do we, Beatrice?"

"No," said Beatrice quietly, and as he looked at her expectantly, she raised her voice a little more and repeated, "No, we don't."

They listened to the wind for a moment. "What does she say now?" Ned said, at last.

"She's quiet," said Beatrice.

"And you?" Ned turned towards her, held out his hand and tugged her to her feet. "What do *you* say?"

Beatrice looked at him for a long moment, at the sheen of tears in his grey eyes, the excited flush in his cheeks, his chest that was still rapidly rising and falling. In the end, the only words she could summon were words from the past.

"Would you like to kiss me?" she asked. "I'll let you, to say sorry for making you cry."

EPILOGUE

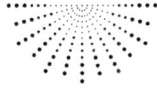

The young woman called Beatrice Morgan had had more names in her life than most people. Each change of name had involved a transformation of some kind. The orphan had become the unwelcomed responsibility of an aunt, then a rich lady's ward, then the wife of a gambler, then a waitress at a gin-house, and then, for a few short years, she became something in-between: just herself, whatever that meant. After their meeting at the graveyard, she had gone back with Ned to Mr Perry's office, where there had followed a long and painful discussion about all the secrets that had been kept from her. She learned that Aunt Martha, whom she had thought never cared for her, had tried to find her after she ran away, and that Mrs Simpson had hidden the truth from her.

Ned and Beatrice had not cast out her spirit for good that day in the graveyard, much as they might have hoped it was so. Mrs Simpson went on making her presence known in their lives in unexpected ways. There were many more secrets that she had kept – lies that she had told – and jokes that she had played upon the people around her, which revealed themselves as the years passed. They would never really be rid of her. Perhaps it was partly for that reason that Beatrice decided to keep the first name that Mrs Simpson had given her – perhaps this was also because the name 'Felicity' held just as many painful associations for her as the name 'Beatrice'.

What Ned had done, that day in Southgate under the swirling snow, was to show Beatrice that even if Mrs Simpson's voice would always reside in her head, she could choose to ignore it. There were always better things that she could give her attention to: the things she loved, for instance, music and drawing; the people she loved, a list which was beginning to include Ned's name, and the people who needed her. This last category was one with which Beatrice became more familiar when she began to volunteer at the soup-kitchen that had saved her on that winter's morning. She went back to the church sometimes too, even though it was quite far from her new lodgings in Holborn. The walk was worthwhile, just to talk to her friend the minister.

At one time in her young life, Beatrice had thought of herself at the top of the world. Her expectations had been piled so high, because of the carelessness of people around her and because of her own weaknesses, that they had been designed to be toppled. Beatrice would never reach those dizzying heights again. But, left to her own devices for the first time, she began to form her own opinions and beliefs. In the house in Highgate, she had been exposed to the same small set of people on a daily basis. Now, the sheer variety of people who passed through her life – some bad, some good, some in between – made her see that there was something miraculous about being on earth after all. It was one short step from there to the kind of belief that she had scorned all her life, the kind of belief that her friend the minister had urged already existed within her in some form.

And although it had sometimes seemed that the world was against her – although, when she had first left James, things had only seemed to go from bad to worse – Beatrice soon found herself with great cause to be thankful, when the single greatest mistake of her life was erased, and she was allowed to start again as Miss Smith. Anxious to secure Miss Simpson as soon as possible, Mr Morgan applied for an annulment of his and Beatrice's marriage instead of a divorce, and his application was accepted, helped by the fact that he and Beatrice had lived apart for the previous three months. He and Miss Simpson were married shortly thereafter, and Beatrice was not invited to the wedding, although Ned Hyland *was*. Ned carried back a report to Beatrice of how extravagant the ceremony and reception had been, upon which they were both able to agree that the five thousand pounds left to the new Mrs Morgan was not likely to last very long.

Upon getting the annulment, Beatrice's thoughts did not immediately turn to marriage. In her newly-varied acquaintance, there were certainly some young men who captured her attention, though none as ardent or as patient as Ned. Swept up by her fresh, youthful beauty, they would imagine that she had had no trials or ordeals to fix her opinions, and any signs to the contrary would usually disturb them. Because she was not what these men had imagined at first, she would therefore prove a disappointment. But often the disappointment was on her side, too, for her experience with Mr Morgan had taught her to look past appearances, and nowadays, when a man set out to charm her, she was on her guard. Usually that charm hid some weakness of their own: a roving eye or an incapacity to feel very deeply.

Ned, all this time, had been true to his word. He was happy being Beatrice's friend, or at least gave every appearance of being so. They saw each other most days. Ned had gotten a new job as a counting clerk, and his hours were more flexible now than they had been in the insurance company. He might meet Beatrice for lunch, or a walk in the park in the evening, or a visit to the shops on Saturday. Sometimes, they could stand in a bookseller's for hours without exchanging a single word; other times, sitting together in an inn or eating house, they would have so much to say to each other that the food on their plates would end up getting cold.

The only days that Beatrice did not see Ned at all were when he was shut up in his lodgings, working on some article or other. She was therefore secure in the conviction that there were no other young women taking up his time – and all the more secure once Miss Matilda Low, who anyone could see had eyes for Ned, ended up marrying his friend Frank Allen instead. But after Mr Low's treatise on the working-class in Ireland and Britain ended up selling better than anyone had anticipated, a sequel was commissioned. Since Ned and Frank had supplied many of the interviews in the book, a sequel meant another tour and another set of interviews, this time across mainland Europe. Ned, between his salary and the shared royalties of Mr Low's book, was able to finance his own tour this time. He disappeared from Beatrice's life for four months, only showing himself occasionally in the smudged writing of a postcard or hasty letter.

Beatrice began to feel, then, something like a stomach-ache that wouldn't go away. For a while she really feared she might be ill. Days somehow seemed longer than they ever had before. She would often visit Mr Perry's office, ostensibly on business – for it was Mr Perry who, to make up for his part in Beatrice's deception, now paid her a small allowance – but really to hear if there were any updates on Ned.

When the tour was finally over, Beatrice's discomfort was increased in hearing that, as soon as his boat had landed back on English shores, Ned had gone straight to Durham to see his family. She knew that, over the last few years, he had been trying to mend things with his father after they had a falling out over Ned's choice of profession. But still she couldn't understand why he wouldn't have stopped in London first. She felt furious at him for caring about something else more than her. Then, all at once, the misery of the last few months attained a new clarity, and Beatrice realised the danger she was in.

By the time Ned showed up at her lodgings in Holborn, a full fortnight after he had returned to England, Beatrice had accepted her fate. She stepped into the parlour of her boarding house and he sprang to his feet to greet her. His face was newly-tanned and his grey eyes held a kind of distant look in them that Beatrice had seen before. She came forward swiftly and put her arms around him, and held him for a long time.

"Don't ever go away again," Beatrice ordered when she pulled away, looking up to note, with satisfaction, that the distant look was gone from Ned's eyes.

"But I might have to," he said, apologetically. "You see, I have a new project – a book of my own, that I've been working on. Not a political book but a novel. And I may have to travel to finish the research for it: I don't want to write about a place I have never been. It wouldn't seem right. So you see..."

"Very well," said Beatrice, who was still holding him. "Then, the next time you go away, please bring me with you."

Ned opened his mouth as if to argue back and then looked down at her, startled, as though he had just realised what she had said. "You know what that would mean."

Beatrice assured him that she did, and after that there was not much more discussion on the question between them. No one who knew them was surprised to hear of their engagement; the only wonder seemed to be that it had taken them so long. It was 1860 when Beatrice Smith changed her name once again, but this time for reasons that were rather less complicated, and in anticipation of a transformation that, if rather more every day, was sure to be a happy one.

～

THANK YOU FOR CHOOSING A PUREREAD BOOK!

We hope you enjoyed the story, and as a way to thank you for choosing PureRead we'd like to send you this free book, and other fun reader rewards…

Click here for your free copy of Whitechapel Waif
PureRead.com/victorian

Thanks again for reading.
See you soon!

LOVE VICTORIAN ROMANCE?

If you enjoyed this story why not continue straight away with other books in our PureRead Victorian Romance library?

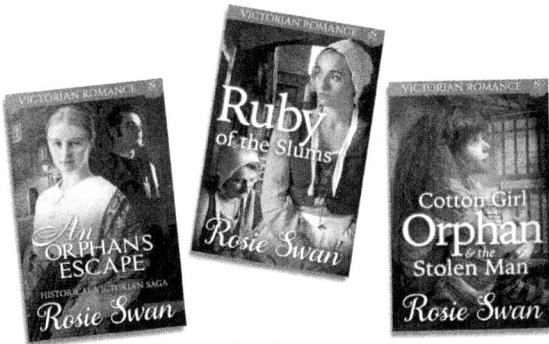

Read them all...

Orphan Christmas Miracle

An Orphan's Escape

The Lowly Maiden's Loyalty

Ruby of the Slums

The Dancing Orphan's Second Chance

Cotton Girl Orphan & The Stolen Man

Victorian Slum Girl's Dream

The Lost Orphan of Cheapside

Dora's Workhouse Child

Saltwick River Orphan

Workhouse Girl and The Veiled Lady

OUR GIFT TO YOU

AS A WAY TO SAY THANK YOU WE WOULD LOVE TO SEND YOU THIS BEAUTIFUL STORY FREE OF CHARGE.

Our Reader List is 100% FREE

Click here for your free copy of Whitechapel Waif

PureRead.com/victorian

At PureRead we publish books you can trust. Great tales without smut or swearing, but with all of the mystery and romance you expect from a great story.

Be the first to know when we release new books, take part in our fun competitions, and get surprise free books in your inbox by signing up to our Reader list.

As a thank you you'll receive an exclusive copy of Whitechapel Waif - a beautiful book available only to our subscribers...

Click here for your free copy of Whitechapel Waif

PureRead.com/victorian

Printed in Dunstable, United Kingdom

66177619R00160